# Also by Chris Lynch

Gypsy Davey

Iceman

Shadow Boxer

Slot Machine

Extreme Elvin

Political Timber

Blue-Eyed Son #1 — Mick

Blue-Eyed Son #2 — Blood Relations

Blue-Eyed Son #3 — Dog Eat Dog

# WHITECHURCH

## CHRIS LYNCH

**HarperCollins**Publishers

Grateful acknowledgment is made
for permission to reprint the following:
Lyrics from "Saturday Night at the Movies." Words and music by
Barry Mann and Cynthia Weil. Copyright © 1964 (Renewed)
Screen Gems-EMI Music Inc. All rights reserved.
International Copyright Secured. Used by permission.

For information address HarperCollins Publishers,
1350 Avenue of the Americas, New York, NY 10019.
www.harpercollins.com

Library of Congress Cataloging-in-Publication Data
Lynch, Chris.
    Whitechurch / Chris Lynch.
       p.     cm.
    Summary: Describes the stresses and strains in the triangular rela-
tionship of two aimless teenage boys and a girl living in a small town.
    ISBN 0-06-028330-0. — ISBN 0-06-028331-9 (lib. bdg.)
    ISBN 0-06-447143-8 (pbk.)
    [1. Interpersonal relations—Fiction.    2. City and town life—
Fiction.]    I. Title.
PZ7.L979739Wh    1999                                    98-54799
[Fic]—dc21                                                  CIP
                                                            AC

Typography by Hilary Zarycky
❖
First paperback edition, 2000

*For Walker and Sophia*
*The Sun and the Moon*

# Contents

# KISS

Kiss me.
Kiss me good-bye.
Plant the kiss like you plant
the seed
and something grows.
Daffodils
Lillies
deviltries.
Wrong.
You think you are a poet
because you write poetry.
You think you are not
because you do not.

John Donne thought
death died
and people didn't.
Ecclesiastes' Preacher said
find the good
enjoy your stay
but when your time comes
be on your way.
I knew a lady who loved them both
to death.
But not you. You and death
don't mix.
Rasputin, you are,
living
while I think I tried to kill you
every chance I got.
Because you have
a frightening will
to live.
That I don't share,
cannot bear.
Wrong.
To me
you would be
too needy

to endure
anymore.

Wrong.
It was not you,
but what you knew.
That life
and its accomplices
are much more
than we'd planned for.
And we need help,
so you held my hand
never figuring
the devil's clasp
would be that warm.

Spin the barrel
pull the trigger
kiss the wrong person.
All hell breaks loose.
Get thee behind me, Satan,
and stay there.
The only thing
that never stops making sense
is

Do unto others.
Peach-colored girls
and willowy bibliarians
and raw-boned she
who should be your sister.
Flail around
grabbing for embracing
clutching air
because it isn't there.

Beguile
bedevil
be gone.
He loved
loved
loved
Do unto others.
Until
It was done unto him.
His smile relieved
and we received.
He is not a gifted poet,
he is a gift.
Which we returned.
Kiss me Pauly.
We got it all wrong.

# COCKED & LOCKED

"TELL ME, OAKLEY," PAULY SAYS.

"I will, Pauly," I say right back. "I'll tell you just as soon as you ask. But that's the way questions work, you have to ask me something first. Then I can tell you."

He'll do that if you don't stay on him. He'll float you a question without ever asking it, till you want to choke it out of him. He says he's a poet. Which, he says, explains everything.

I don't think it does. Nothing explains everything.

We are perched on the slope of a small green hill overlooking my buddy Pauly's most favorite of all favorite places in Whitechurch. The prison. There's some milling about going on in the yard, but since this is Thursday afternoon, it's not the prisoners doing the milling, but guards and police and prison officials practicing their fife-and-drum stuff.

They're god-awful. We never miss it.

"Okay," Pauly says. "Just a what-if. What if, if a guy wanted to pick one off. You think somebody could do that, and get away with it?"

"A cop? Pauly, you asking me if you could shoot a cop and nobody would mind?"

"Of course not," he says, sticking a sharp elbow into my side. "You think I'm a dope?"

A lot of times I do, I do think he's a dope. But I don't ever say it to him. He's heard it enough, I figure.

"No," Pauly continues. "I mean, a con. What if somebody got the idea to drop a prisoner, right down there in the yard? Would anybody really mind, do you think?"

I turn toward Pauly to see if he's joking, but there isn't a joke anywhere in him. He keeps staring down at the yard.

"Ya, Pauly. I think somebody'd mind. Probably, somebody'd mind a lot."

Pauly waits a long time, staring off, listening to the fife and drum—and bagpipe, actually—strangle some innocent song to death.

"I don't see why," Pauly says. "I really don't think people would care much."

In the yard below us, the leader of the police group is screaming and throwing his baton against the twenty-foot-high fence. Like he does every week.

"Of *course* you're bored," he yells at the pipers. "We only know the one goddamn song.

Who the hell wants to play 'Loch Lomond' fifteen hundred times? Ya bunch a dopes."

Pauly's eyes narrow. "What about him?" he
asks, pointing at the yeller.

"They might not care much," I sigh, "but
they'd still notice."

"See, that's what I think about the criminals.
I think maybe people would notice if you did one
of them, you'd get noticed for it, but in the end,
nobody'd get pissed off about it. Which would be
kind of slick in the end, don't you think?"

## LILLY #7

she's LEAving me red

VIolence is blue

WHITEchurch is brown

there's a fuckin ROCK in my shoe


by pauLY


Pauly was always fascinated with the prison,
since the first cinder block was laid for it. Matter
of fact, everybody was into it, when the building
was going up and it seemed like every last person
in the area was either working on it or selling
donuts or Coors to those who were. At that time,
it was a very popular prison.

Then they went and filled it all up with criminals. Spoiled everything.

Then they went and named it.

Whitechurch Prison. Made sense to me.

"An appallingly shortsighted and insensitive decision," was what they called it on the editorial page of the *Whitechurch Spire*.

People, apparently, are very sensitive to words and word use and they are far more sensitive to words when they are written down. Because it never bothered anybody during the building stage or the dedication stage or the opening-up stage when officials would refer to the place as Whitechurch Prison. It only finally bothered folks when it came down in the papers, and criminals started getting directed to come spend time in our jail, and the newspaper writers started shorthanding things.

"The murderer was sentenced to life in Whitechurch."

"With time served and good behavior, the prisoner could be allowed to leave Whitechurch by the time he is ninety-seven years old."

And on like that. It was funny, really, if you could see it. Pauly went right out and had sweatshirts made up for the two of us, white stencil lettering on black: PROPERTY OF WHITECHURCH PRISON. Most locals didn't care for the humor.

"Whitechurch is, and has been for nearly three hundred years," the editorial read, "one of the most picturesque and tranquil villages in the entire Northeast. It is a fine and wonderful town, and no one has to be 'sentenced' to Whitechurch."

He was right about the picturesque part, as long as you didn't come during mud season, and as long as you didn't point your camera in the direction of the Gleasons' yard. But tranquil?

Tranquil. We'd have to chew on that one a little bit. We'd have to define our terms very specifically, wouldn't we, and make a clear distinction between what went on above the surface and what went on underneath.

"Don't you ever get angry, Oakley?"

This is Lilly, who is smiling and who is Pauly's girlfriend, even though she spends way more time with me than she does with him. She's big and dark and quite special if you pay close enough attention. She's possibly plain if you don't. We're together this March afternoon, hanging out and finding out, up on the faraway hill next to the cider-press building that wouldn't be pressing anything until the next leaf-peeping busload came by in the fall. This particular press is located on this particular hill because this is the best-looking spot for people to overspy our little kingdom while they sip their fresh juices. The view down Press Hill is what we want to look like. Cider is what we want to taste like.

Pauly hates apples so much, you'd think they were a disease. "Of course I get angry," I answer Lilly. "What kind of a question is that?"

"It's a regular question, is all. Because if you do get angry, it's angry in a way I can't see."

And Lilly likes to be able to see all. Lilly likes

things in plain sight where she can see them.

"You mean, like Pauly gets angry?" I ask her. The question I'm not supposed to ask. That's why I'm special to her, because I don't usually ask.

"Don't, Oakley," she says, and starts down the hill. I start after her.

"Fine, then, I won't," I say. "Come on back up the hill with me. I'll behave and be quiet."

She comes back up the hill and sits beside me again. "I have to go in a few minutes anyway," she tells me. "Baby-sitting for the Rev."

I nod, which is my best thing. I sit, and I behave. Because there is nothing I like better than sitting on the hill doing nothing on a nice day while Lilly sits close beside me doing nothing too. Some guys—like Pauly, and a lot of the older guys at the high school—don't seem to appreciate this, doing nothing. But that's not me. I'm doing all the nothing I can while I can because I can feel it coming, the day when I have to do *something*.

But then, for no reason, I make the trouble again.

"So, what does he do, Lilly?" I ask. "You want to tell me what he does when he's angry with you?"

And that's that. Without speaking, she gets up, brushes old yellow grass off her seat, and heads down the hill, down straight toward the white church of Whitechurch, where the Reverend and his wife and their baby live in the shadow of the valley.

I know I've done it—exploded the good thing we have up on Press Hill—and I don't even try to make good. I just follow along behind Lilly as she breaks into a jog down the decline, and before we reach the Texaco at the foot, she will have let me catch up.

"Yo," comes the holler from back up where we just left.

Pauly, of course.

"Stop right there, you two," he yells, pointing down on us like Moses or somebody.

There has been, really, nothing between me and Lilly, and Pauly knows it. Nothing but being friends, anyway. It was just that if Pauly was your best friend like he is with me, or if he was your boyfriend like he is with her, then you'd find yourself needing somebody else to talk to on a regular basis.

I'm that for Lilly, and she's that for me. Pauly doesn't care at all, the way a lot of guys would if their best friends seemed to be bird-dogging their girls. In fact, he seems to enjoy the setup.

"You, and you, come over here to me right this minute," Pauly says, pointing at the piece of Press Hill right in front of him.

I'm staring at him, thinking of walking back up there, when Lilly grabs my hand and yanks me along, laughing like a mad thing. We speed, like a couple of boulders hurtling down the steep grade, until I'm sure I'm going to lose it and wind up with a mouth full of turf.

Pauly tries a little, screaming and chasing us

a short ways, but he doesn't have a chance. Everybody is faster than Pauly.

At the Reverend's house, Lilly and I are sitting on the sofa across from the window seat in the curved alcove that looks out over the yard. The baby is sleeping. The baby is always sleeping. We are watching a movie on cable, but not really watching it. I do this thing—and I think Lilly does it too, but to ask would be to shatter it—where I watch the famous stars on the TV screen, but I don't listen to a thing they say, and I don't think at all about what's happening to them in the plot. For soundtrack, I listen to Lilly, and to myself, and we and the stars mesh all up together.

"If your life was a movie, who would star in it?" Lilly asks me as she passes the tortilla chips.

I've only thought about this a hundred thousand times, but that doesn't make the answer come any quicker. The players keep changing, most of them.

"Sean Connery would play my father," I say as I pass her my Coke.

Lilly slaps me on the arm and says, "That's not a real answer," while she laughs.

"Well they're both bald, aren't they?" I say.

"All right, Connery plays your father. Who plays you, then?"

I nod confidently. "Pierce Brosnan," I say. "It's perfect, 'cause we're already like a father-son pair of double-oh-seven action types."

Lilly snatches the chips back from me. "Interesting, when you think about it, Oakley," she says. "Maybe we should explore your family dynamics a little more."

"Maybe not," I say. "So who's in *your* movie?"

"Audrey Hepburn," Lilly says. "But when she was alive, of course. Like in *Wait Until Dark*, where she was blind."

Lilly isn't blind. Unless she really believes she looks like Audrey Hepburn. She's more like two Audrey Hepburns, but that isn't important at all. The stuff that makes her someone you want to get next to is mostly invisible, Lilly stuff.

## LILLY #31

If Violence is blue

and my lilly is pink

which Motion would move her

which Potion should I drink?

"What about him?" I ask, pointing across the room, over the window seat, through the window and out into the backyard where our Pauly dances up and down for our amusement. Pauly's forbidden to enter the Reverend's house. He's got a good soul in there somewhere, the Rev says, but he's never going to cross *this* threshold. Whatever that means.

"So who plays him?" I ask again.

Pauly rushes up to the window, climbs up on the woodpile, and presses his face to the glass.

"Pauly's not going to be in my movie," Lilly says seriously.

I wave to him. "Hey, Pauly," I say.

"Go ahead," he calls, muffled, through the glass. "Go on and kiss her if you want to."

"I never said I wanted to," I reply, all indignant. I'm not fooling anyone, though.

"Hey," Lilly snaps. "What do you two think you're doing? Trading at the farmers' market or something? I'm a *human*, Pauly-the-Pig. Get out of here."

"No, wait," he says. "I want to show you something, Lilly. Come here."

"I don't want another poem. They make me ill."

"Hey, I said I was a poet. I never said I was a *gifted* poet. Anyway, it's not a poem. It's something better, even."

"I don't want *that*, either. I *especially* don't want that. And if you try to show it to me again, I'll call the Reverend."

"It's not that either," Pauly says, exasperated.

I'm starting to get a little embarrassed. "Maybe I should go."

"No, you absolutely shouldn't," she says to me.

Pauly. "Just come to the window, Lilly."

Lilly. "Ignore him, Oakley."

Me. "How can you ignore Pauly? How can anyone ignore Pauly?"

Lilly. "Easy."

Pauly. "Not anymore, it ain't. I'm going to be unignorable. C'mere."

Lilly sighs, turns up the sound on the TV with the remote.

"Well, I'm going to go look," I say. She shrugs.

When I'm almost to the window, and Pauly is reaching down into his pants, the sound of the Reverend's car on the gravel driveway pulls Pauly's attention like a scared deer listening on the wind. And like a deer, he is gone in an instant, into the trees and out of sight.

"He's been getting weirder and weirder since I told him about the college," Lilly says, shaking her head at the silent-again television.

## LILLY #50

Girl sits with boy but doesn't never

really talk

Like her mouth's been all taped

and stuffed

with a sock

she'll think of him well though

when he's outlined

in chalk

or when some body's brain cells

are splashed

on a rock


"Think she'll like it?" he asks me.

I don't know what to say. Everybody always says that, but here I am totally true about it. I have no idea what to tell him.

"You mean the poem?"

"No, stupid, I know she's going to like the poem. It's my best work."

In that case, he must mean the other thing.

"So, what do you think?"

What I think is, I think I might fall down right here, my knees are so weak.

"I think, get that away from me, Pauly, that's what I think."

"Ah, ya big baby. It's not gonna hurt you. Look, she's cocked and locked here, so she looks ready to fire, but she won't."

*She* being the Colt.

"I thought Colt 45 was a drink," I say as I take a few steps backward, toward the cider press.

Pauly follows me, chuckling. "You're funny, Oak. Here, check it out."

As if I could *avoid* checking it out. It is the same shape as the state of Texas, with the barrel pointing north, the hammer pointing west, the handle sticking down into Mexico's side, and the shooter's knuckles scraping along from

Louisiana to Oklahoma.

Nearly as big as Texas too. When skinny old Pauly waves the thing around, it pulls his arm along like he's not in charge of it at all.

"That's okay," I say, "I can see it fine."

"You can't see it. You gotta *feel* it, is the thing, Oakley."

He grabs my wrist and works the monster into my palm. My hand closes around it, and it nearly pulls me to the ground.

"She's gonna go 'wow,'" Pauly says.

"She's gonna go *something*," I say. I can feel my free hand shaking as I examine the Colt up close.

But Pauly is right about this: It's unignorable.

It's like, every line is in place. Every straight is straight, every curve is *schwoop*, it's cool to the touch but feels so comfortable in the fleshy innermost of the palm that you feel as if it knows what it's doing, and it probably belongs there. The barrel is polished blue-gray, almost the same color as the late-afternoon light behind the hill, and the brilliant stainless steel body catches every chip of that light and forces you to pay close attention.

Automatically, like a five-year-old, I raise it up, close one eye, and point it. At an apple tree. At a squirrel.

"Where'd you get it?" I ask.

"Really want to know?"

I look up at my friend's face, to see whether in fact I do. He smiles crookedly. I don't.

"Borrowed it from the Rev's collection that he doesn't want nobody to know about. He knows *I* know, though."

I knew I didn't want to know.

"She's leaving because of me, because I'm boring her," Pauly says.

I aim at the little rusted rooster twisting on top of the cider-press house. "Pauly, you are many things—in fact, you're *most* things I can think of to call somebody—but one thing you could never be is boring."

"Well, we know that, but I think Lilly is bored with me, and that's why she's leaving Whitechurch."

"She's leaving Whitechurch to go to school. If the university was here, she wouldn't be leaving."

"That's just an excuse," he says.

Lilly is where she's supposed to be. Pauly told her to meet him. I'm not where I'm supposed to be. I'm not supposed to be here at all. But when Lilly told me he wanted her to meet him at our spot above the prison yard, I decided I should be here. It's Wednesday afternoon, and as we wait for Pauly, we listen to the fife-and-drum-and-bagpipe corps. They've been getting better. They've got "Loch Lomond" pretty well nailed.

But they're not supposed to be here. It's not Thursday.

"Sounds so pretty," Lilly says. "How come you guys never told me about this before? This is sweet."

I nod. She looks nervous, no matter what she says.

"Did he tell you what he wanted you up here for?"

"Said he wants to show me something. But he's always saying that. To tell you the truth, he hasn't really shown me anything in a long time."

I let out a low, steady whistle, the kind that everybody knows means "Oh, boy."

"Well what can I say, Oakley? You understand, I know you do. There's nothing wrong with what I'm doing."

Of course I understand. The Lilly-Pauly relationship was always the type of thing that practically brought "Booooo" calls from the whole town. The Reverend, for one, would carry her on his back to Boston, with all her luggage, to get her away from him.

"He'll be okay," I say, and I have never said a more outrageous thing. "In fact, you probably don't even have to wait for him now. I'll talk to him. He'll be—"

"What the hell are *they* doing down there," Pauly says, popping up behind us quiet as a catamount. He walks right on past us and points down at the prison yard with the Colt.

"My god, Pauly," Lilly gasps. We both jump to our feet. "What is that?"

"They are not supposed to be there," he insists. "This isn't Thursday. Is it? Oakley, is this Thursday?"

I start to answer, but he cuts me off.

"And *you're* not supposed to be here, either. This was supposed to be a special moment between me and my girl."

He is gesturing at me with it now. But he doesn't mean anything by it.

"Don't call me your girl, Pauly. I don't like that."

It is my turn to gasp. "Do you *see* what he's holding, Lillian? Maybe you could save this conversation—"

"I'm very worried about you leaving," he says. "You need me, Lilly, we all know that. I can make you happy, Lil."

Lilly shakes her head.

"Listen," I say. "She's not even leaving for months, yet. Why don't we save all this, okay? We have the spring and the summer still and it'll be the same . . . it'll be better, even, than all the others. Then, next year when Pauly and me graduate, we'll come down and join you and everything will be back—"

"I can make you happy, Lilly," he repeats. "We all know that. You're just a little bored with things right now, you want a little—"

"Pauly," she says calmly, but not without a little tremor in there. "Pauly . . ." She doesn't seem to know how to finish.

Pauly wheels around to face the small figures down in the prison yard again. He's staring. I hear the distinctive *click-click* of the hammer pulling back.

"Cocked, Pauly, huh?" I say. "Locked?"

He pauses for a long time. He nods. "Cocked and locked."

Pauly doesn't want to hurt anybody. I know Pauly doesn't want to hurt anybody. Lilly knows it too. We're probably the two people in town who know. In the fall, there'll only be one.

He turns back to face us, and as he does he aims straight up into the cloudless azure blue of the sky. The Colt blends with it, with the blue, as if it were a siphon, drinking blue down out of the air, down through the polished blue muzzle, through the faded blue arm of Pauly's old fleece-lined denim jacket, and into the blue body of pale Paul himself. Feeding into him, so much bigger than him.

"Do you see this?" he asks her. "Don't you *see* this, Lilly?"

"I do," she says. "Does it lead us to something, Pauly?"

We all wait on that. We wait more out of courtesy than fear, to give him a chance to withdraw with dignity.

"You need me" is all he can manage. He uncocks.

With that, Lilly turns and walks away, leaving Paul with his hand still stuck in the air. He stares at her back for an awfully long time.

I don't turn to watch Lilly leave, because I don't stop watching Pauly. But I can see by the draining of his face when she has cleared out of sight.

"You're not leaving me, though, are you,

Oakley?" he asks, lowering the Colt finally.

"Of course I'm not leaving you."

He turns back toward the prison and sits down cross-legged in the dirt.

I sit next to him. "Somebody would notice," I remind him. "And it wouldn't be a good notice."

Pauly finally smiles. He leans a shoulder into me, tipping me over onto the ground.

"Ah, autumn's still ages away, huh, Oak?"

"Ya," I say, propping up on one elbow. "Ages away."

"Ages away," he says.

Then Pauly puts the nozzle of the Colt in his mouth. He has to open his jaws all the way to fit the thing in there.

I stay frozen to the ground. While I do, and while Pauly remains likewise still, he rolls just his eyes in my direction. When he's had a good look at my stricken face, the smile comes back to him again. He looks like a skeleton with the pistol in his teeth.

"Almost looked sick there, buddy," he says as he pulls it out.

"Almost was," I say.

"That's good," he says. "That's good." He stands, and offers me a hand. "We can go home now," he says.

When he's got me halfway to my feet, he drops me. I'm on the seat of my pants. He comes right up close to me.

"Put this in your mouth," he says coolly.

I say nothing. I feel the blood-warmth run out of my face like a flushing toilet. The big hole at the tip of the Colt is now pressed like a cold mouth against mine.

"Go ahead now, Oakley. Do what I tell you."

I open up, and my friend doesn't hesitate before easing the barrel in, the sight scraping along the roof of my mouth. Pauly pulls back on the hammer, and it sounds like the mechanism is clacking and clacking, tumbling like the lock on a gigantic steel vault.

"What does it taste like?" he asks. "It tastes blue, don't you think?"

Of course, I can't answer.

"Not nervous, are you? Oak? Of course not. Cocked and locked, right?"

There is another click.

"Cocked . . . unlocked," he says, grinning. "Did I tell you how sensitive the Colt .45 semi-automatic is? I didn't? Oh, let me then. When it's cocked and unlocked, this piece will fire if you *tell* it to fire."

There is nothing for me to do, then, except keep on looking up into Pauly's tired, watery eyes. So I keep on. Until finally I see, in there, where *my* Pauly is, and he looks back at me.

He blinks away some of the glaze.

Slowly, gingerly, I back off. *Remove* myself from the gun.

He points it into the dirt and uncocks it.

"You're my friend, Oakley," he says.

"I am," I say.

He raises the Colt again, points it in my face. "If I tell you to put this back in your mouth once more, are you still my friend?"

I open my mouth as wide as I can.

Pauly puts the gun in my hand and closes his eyes.

"I'm going to write you a poem," he says. "'Oakley #1.'"

I tug on his jacket and start him down the hill.

"You do and I'll shoot ya," I say, and this brightens his mood considerably.

# Love Me Don't

**I** LOVED HER FIRST.

She showed up in town about one month before the end of the school year, plunked down into the seat next to me after spending the previous eight months in a seat somewhere else next to someone else.

His loss, I figured, and I still remember that, thinking that, right that first day. His loss, who-ever he was. I never considered that maybe she hadn't even sat next to a boy at all, because that would have lessened my victory. His loss, my gain. I would think those kinds of thoughts end-lessly, my unearned triumphs over life, watching the constellation of dust particles floating before my face while the lessons of the day would float past my ears. By the next September they'd bumped her up a year ahead of me where she belonged, but I did have that one sweet month.

"Kind of late in the year for a move, isn't it?"
I said instead of learning why humans could
stand on their heads and still swallow food into
their stomachs. "Or early. Must've been pretty
important, for your family to move you right in
the—"

"Must've been," Lilly said, and smiled at me.
Then she did this thing, this sort of snake
charmer maneuver that I don't think she did on
purpose exactly, but that she did very well all the
same. She leaned a little closer to me and stared
into my eyes with this look that was like bits and
pieces of question and sympathy, of asking for-
giveness and offering it at the same time. A slight
tilting of the head, a narrowing of the eyes, down
turned the corners of her mouth as up went the
center. It was the look that defined, and defines,
our interactions.

"If I ask you not to ask me about that, will
you not?"

Something in there, and the way she said it,
gave me a little shake. I still think about that
sometimes. How tidy and useful a motto that is.
If I ask you not . . . will you not?

"Okay," I said, even though of course she
only made me ten times as curious.

She shook my hand then. And we were
friends.

Her grip was firm, like a man's is supposed to
be, and honest. Like she wasn't selling me something or showing me how strong she was, or
picking my pocket with her free hand. Her grip

was firm and warm. Not all girl, was what I thought when Lilly first gripped me like that. Not all girl, and not at all guy.

That's how it started, believe it or not. Lilly and Pauly. Lilly and me and Pauly.

We were thirteen and fourteen. Not that we were both at the same time. Lilly was fourteen and Pauly and I were thirteen and, as a bona fide legal working-age teenager, she got a summer job, making money and listening to music and eating ice cream.

The actual job of ice-cream man's assistant belonged to her, but she brought me along because we were already doing our thing of doing things together. She was still pretty new, and after that promising start in buddying up to me, she sort of stalled out and was never surrounded by tons of friends. I liked to think that she figured I was enough. But then I'd come down and think no, I was the best she could do. Whatever, I was happy enough with the situation, and didn't care whether or not I got paid while hanging around Lil.

Stan the ice-cream man didn't care much either. He was about six foot two, with long superfine white hair and pink eyes and purple tattoos. Half a smile, too. Right side. The right side of his smile could smile but the left couldn't because he fell off his bike and onto his face during his previous career as a stoned paperboy.

"Who are you?" he said as Lilly led me by the hand up into the truck that first morning.

"He's my buddy," Lilly said, standing in front of me protectively.

Stan started the truck. "Well buddy don't get paid. But what the hell . . ." He shrugged and flipped a switch, and we hit the road to the tinkly tune of "Here We Go Round the Mulberry Bush."

"You are so lucky," I said after an hour of doing not much of anything. "I mean, this is it. You have it all. Died and gone to heaven. This is, like, the most perfect thing I ever saw, like, you should just do this for the rest of your life, Lilly, 'cause it's never gonna get any better than this."

She looked at me with The Look. "Oakley, you are just messing with me, right? I mean, like, you have bigger dreams than *this*, don't you?"

You know how, after you've said something, you know the rightness or wrongness of it by what you hear in somebody else's voice? I had to scramble then, because the truth was I'd meant what I said. I thought this ice-cream truck was the living end. I had already settled into my groove of "Think small, or not at all."

"Well, Lil, y'know, a lot of kids would kill for this. You get free ice cream, listen to music all day, get paid, and—

"Hey, Lilly, you wanna drive?" Stan hollered back over his shoulder.

All I could do was point at him. He had said it all for me.

"Okay," Lilly said, laughing, "it's a pretty good job." Then she put her hand on my shoulder and spoke close to my face and way down deep into me. Like she does still. "But there is lots more, Oak. You know there is. And if I thought you meant what you were saying, I might cry right here in front of the ice creams and everything."

I looked at her. I looked at Stan.

"And bring us some strawberry shortcakes and Mountain Dews," he sang.

I shook my head at her. "Okay. How 'bout if I wanted to *own* the ice-cream truck, would that be better?"

"You are very funny, Oakley," she said.

I was quite unaware of being funny. I'd say that most people were unaware of my being funny. Lilly found me funny.

I stood with my back against the windshield, in the big empty space up front, while Stan and Lilly shared the large driver's seat and the driving. Lilly was beaming. The steering wheel was oversized, big even for a full-grown man and almost silly on Lilly, like she was captaining a ship. She was completely confident, though, and game. They took turns controlling the steering, while Stan did the pedals. When Lilly's ice cream started to melt down her arm, she took a break.

I stood there and watched Lilly, while Lilly sat there, licked her ice cream, and watched Stan and his footwork. She was preparing to work the pedals.

"Is this a good living, Stan?" Lilly wanted to know.

Stan laughed loudly. "It's crap." He took a
long pull on his Mountain Dew, beeped the horn,
and waved as he drove right past a five-year-old
waving a dollar. "Here's some business wisdom,
kids. Never waste your time stopping for singles
unless they are stoned teenagers. Little kid like
that is under orders to buy one damn Popsicle
and bring back the change. I'll waste more in
gas slowing down and starting up again than
I'll make on the sale. But if you got a stoned teenager . . . hell, they'll buy up half the truck and
likely as not forget about their change. One of
them can make your whole day."

"Thanks, Stan," I said.

"So you're really like a serious businessman," Lilly said, and right about now this was
starting to bother me.

Stan appeared to give this some thought.
Tooling down the road, gripping the wheel. Then
smiling. This was the thing, I thought, that made
up for the halfness of his smile. The intensity, and
the frequency. He seemed to find a lot of stuff
grinworthy. "Serious? Businessman? Well I tell
you what. I'll do any damn thing I can get paid
for, so I guess the answer is yes."

A flock of young boys came barreling off a
baseball diamond screaming and waving at the
sound of the truck's music.

"*Now* we're talkin'," Stan said as he yanked
us to the curb.

Lilly and I sprang into action, manning the

window as Stan put his feet up on the dash and lit a cigarette.

"He's cool," she said, handing out a snow cone.

"Ya," I said. "I suppose he is. A little. Cool." I did my job, handling the money.

"Come on, Oak. You have to admire the guy some."

I was a little too busy being jealous of him to admire him. "Some," I allowed.

"I said root beer," one angry young baseball player said, shoving a Dr Pepper back across the stainless-steel counter.

Lilly fixed him up. Got back to important matters. "I mean he's a go-getter. Doing what it takes, making his way. Even though he hasn't gotten all the breaks, like with falling on his face and stuff."

"Ya," I said, trying to ho-hum her into submission. "I guess he's a decent ice-cream man."

"Yup. A go-getter. I'm gonna be like that, Oakley." She paused, then spoke more directly to me, like I needed remedial pep-talking. "I'm going to be go-get. You wanna be go with me?"

"I'm having enough trouble tryin' to be understand you, Lilly."

She laughed. "You're the funniest guy, Oakley."

The baseball players had all been served when one straggler came on up.

"No he's not. I'm the funniest guy," Pauly said.

"She doesn't mean that kind of funny. Scram, Pauly."

He wasn't even looking at me. He knew her from school, but only by sight. They never spoke.

"Do I know you?" he said. He was looking at Lilly, so he could have meant it either way. The straight way, where you ask a person—Lilly—if you've met before. Or the jerky way, where you ask a person—me—to please buzz off. Coulda been both, now that I think of it.

"I've seen you around," Lilly said.

"You don't play baseball," I reminded Pauly.

"I'm just here heckling," he said. "Can I have a Coke please? And a Hoodsie? But only if you have the real Hoodsies, with the wooden spoons. Don't waste my time with those plastic spoons."

Lilly was about to get it when I intervened. "No, you can't."

"Oakley," she snapped, getting the stuff anyway. "Why are you being like that?"

"He's my best friend. I can be like that."

"I thought I was your best friend," Lilly said. A joke that wasn't.

"I'll be your best friend," Pauly said to her.

I had this sudden, mad, sweeping feeling of losing. Of losing big things, of losing everything. Stupid, yes. But very real and very very saddening to me.

Until Lilly started laughing. And my things came right back to me.

"That's so nuts, isn't it? The way we do that? Who ever invented that anyway, *best friends*?"

"Barney Rubble," Pauly said authoritatively.

"Come on, let's go," Stan called from the front.

"Oh, your order," Lilly said to Paul.

"He doesn't have the money to pay for it," I said. "I can tell by the way he asked."

"Stop that now," she scolded me.

"Ya, stop," he said. Then he got his refreshments, made sure to open up both very quickly so we couldn't take them back.

"Buck fifty," I said.

He leaned over the counter, sad, sweet, repentant. "Jeez, I had no idea you people were so expensive. Can I borrow a buck forty?"

Lilly started laughing.

"Don't do that, please," I said to her. My turn to scold. "It'll just make him worse."

"It's fine," Lilly said to Pauly. "Don't listen to him, he doesn't even really work here."

"Come on," Stan said, starting up the truck and cranking the radio. "I finished my cigarette. If we're parked longer than one smoke then we're wasting time."

"Yo, Stan," Pauly called.

"Yo, Pauly," Stan called back. "Don't be comin' around my truck without no money."

"Got it covered," Pauly said confidently, winking at Lilly. I whipped my head around to see if she winked back, but I was too late. Her smile said she had, though.

Off we were, and music blasting, Mountain Dew flowing, we started chatting about you-know-who.

"He's nice," Lilly said.

"No he isn't," I said.

"Really I am, but people don't understand me," Stan said.

Lilly laughed, then excused herself. "Sorry, Stan, we were talking about that boy Pauly, not you. But you're nice too, of course."

"No he isn't," I whispered close by her ear.

It was starting to seem like Lilly found everything I said amusing. She just laughed, shook her head, and slapped my arm.

"Okay, well what about Stan then? You must admit Stan is cool."

"Hell, Lilly, he ain't so great."

"But he is, in his way. He is kind of wild, and at the same time he's serious about stuff. He seems to enjoy himself, and at the same time he pays his bills."

"Even if his bills are probably for heroin or something."

For the moment, she was not amused by me. "What has gotten into you?" she asked.

At which point, I made it worse. "Us," I said. "I get a little jealous, is all."

She covered her mouth with her hand. "Oh," she said softly. "Oh, my . . ."

Which was not what I wanted to hear.

She reached over, lightly touched both of my cheeks with both of her palms. "You can't be my boyfriend, Oakley." She looked desperate, her regular confidence drained away. "I really need you to be more than that. You're my best friend.

You're already my best friend. Ever."

And what, I ask, could I say about that? Has it ever happened, that your ears heard one thing and your heart and lungs and fluttery buttery belly heard a whole different story?

Stan must have felt like he had to say something. "I got a bump on my head, shaped like a number two. Wanna feel it?"

"No," I said.

"Wasn't asking you."

"Sure, I'll feel it," Lilly said. I glared at her, to very little effect.

"Kids!" I hollered, pointing out the window like I was up in the crow's nest of the *Niña*.

"*Rich* kids!" Stan yelled, straightening and pulling the truck right up onto the sidewalk. "Great neighborhood. Next to the stoners, this is my biggest bread-and-butter. Every time I pass through here without my truck somebody calls the cops. Now *that's* a nice neighborhood."

Back at our station.

"You're embarrassing," I said to Lilly as she handed out ices to one polite kid after another. They all wanted napkins. "Don't touch a person's head-bump just because he asks you to. I don't care *what* number it's shaped like."

"Loosen up, will you, Oakley? I was just having fun."

"Ya but, what's he gonna think? When a girl starts feeling the bumps on a guy's head . . . Hey . . . what are you . . . hey, stop laughing at me."

"How old did you say you were, Grandpa?"

I was about to defend myself but came up empty. "Okay," I said, finally getting a small laugh at myself.

"Come on, Oakley, don't you, just for a second, wonder what it would feel like to kiss a mouth like Stan's?" As she said this, she went into a sort of pantomime gimp kiss, tilting her head to the side, trying to do the trick of puckering only half of her mouth.

"Not for a *second*," I said sharply, perhaps underscoring the point about my tightness. "I'll loosen up, but I'm not gonna loosen up that much." I turned away from her, started jamming, forcing change into the children's weak little hands.

Then all at once even these well-mannered, well-entertained kids let out a great collective "Ooohhh," as Lilly kissed long and loud, sloppy and slurpy, on my unguarded cheek.

I stopped moaning, whining, handing out change, and breathing.

"You are funny, and yet you are a bit of a stiff, aren't you," she said into my ear as I stared into the giggly faces before me.

"I may be a stiff, and I may not be your boyfriend, but I can still try to steer you away from freakish guys."

"Too late," Pauly blurted, parting the crowd and practically flopping himself on the counter.

Lilly laughed.

"Wouldja stop laughing at him?" I barked.

"Pauly, for cripes' sake, what are you doing *here* now?"

"Just in the neighborhood," he said, cheesy-smiling at Lilly.

"*This* neighborhood? You got no business in this neighborhood. You got no friends in this neighborhood—"

"Ya, but I got money to pay for my ice cream now," he said, slapping two dollars on the counter. I noticed all the other kids had scrammed. "And I got myself awful thirsty in the process. Howsabout a Coke?"

"My cigarette's nearly out," Stan called, and the truck growled into action. As he looked back our way, Stan fixed Pauly with a stare and, with crack marksmanship, flicked the last of his cigarette at his head.

"Take me with you," Pauly said.

"No," Stan said, putting the truck in gear.

"Then come hang out with me," Paul called, trotting alongside us. "This looks boring as hell anyway."

"Can't," I said.

"Didn't mean you, numbnuts. I meant her."

Lilly marveled at us. "Between the two of you . . . you guys must laugh all day long."

"All day long," I said, and went to sit up with Stan. Lilly hung back to wave to Pauly, as he ran along with the truck.

I watched out of the corner of my unconcerned, unjealous, unboyfriendy eye. Watched Lilly watching Pauly. She liked him, no question, in a way . . . well, in another way. The rat.

Then I looked at the rat himself, chugging along after us like a nutter.

She had every reason in the world to like him. I knew that. Most people didn't. Now Lilly did.

"He says he wrote me a poem," Lilly called to us.

Lilly smiled. Stan did not. Not even a half of a half of a smile. He gunned the engine. Gunning the engine of the Good Humor wagon was not exactly heading into hyperspace, but it was jarring enough, looking at Stan's pale face go pink, listening to the motor strain and groan and slowly overtake the tinkling ice-cream-man music, then the blast of the radio. The whole machine rumbled and shook, made worse by Stan's jagged little jerks of the wheel and inexplicable pattern of gear shifting. I looked back to see black smoke billowing in Pauly's face.

"Can you stop, Stan?" I asked.

"No, I just got it into third—"

"Please," I said, and though he remained in his fringes of society-slanted, hard-guy glower, he worked us back down into second . . . first . . . park.

Pauly was winded but couldn't wait.

### W H A T S E R N A M E  # 1

All day I follow
Bad Humor Man

Freak Albino Burnout

Stan

Just so I can meet

The Girl

Let's just say her name is

Pearl

The one who's gonna change

My Luck

Get close to me

and

lose the Duck


It must have been some serious effort to pull
that off smoothly, because as soon as Pauly finished reciting, he went into spasms of wheezing
and coughing like he would die.

"Come here, come here, come here," Lilly
said, cracking open a Coke and nearly pouring it
into him. Pauly slurped at it like a baby being
bottle-fed. Lilly shook her head as she watched
and, no doubt, replayed the words in her head.

"What *is* it about this town?" she said. "All
these, like, good-sir-knight kind of guys. I never
met anybody like you people. It's like *Camelot*
around here."

"Hey," Stan yelled. "Bad Humor Man Freak
Albino?" He tried to sound mad, but he came off
more like, proud. "I have a very good humor."

"So who's the duck?" I blurted. "Huh,

Pauly? Is that me? I'm the duck then, is that it?"

Pauly started laughing, then wheezing.

"Pearl," Lilly said. "Pearl. That's lovely, isn't it? You're really good at that . . . poetry. Turning ordinary things into special things. That's how it works, isn't it? You are really good. . . ."

"I can't carry you all," Stan said. "If that's where we're headed with this. That's too much."

Paul was catching his breath, and backing away from the truck now.

"No," I said, and got down. "I really don't want to ride anymore." And it was true, I didn't. And besides . . .

"Get up there," I said hard into Pauly's ear.

"I'm coming with you, Oakley," Lilly said.

"No, you have to work. And also . . . you should take this guy. He can't even breathe."

Stan started the truck and jammed it into gear. "Whoever's coming, come now," he said.

"Really?" Lilly mimed to me.

Pauly had no such hesitation. He was already on board and digging around in a cooler.

I went up to her. "You nervous, going with Pauly?"

She shook her head. "Nope. You think he's okay. So he must be okay."

"Yup," I said quietly. "You're gonna love him."

So they saddled up and headed out. I walked along, in the scorching summer sun, enjoying the toasted feeling coming over my face. I closed my eyes to it, continued walking, and listened to the goofy tinkling Good Humor music. I wondered what I had just done.

"Cast thy bread upon the waters . . ." an old comforting voice came back to me.

Until half a block away, Stan skidded to a halt. Out popped Lilly. Walking back my way and waving over her shoulder at the truck. But no Pauly. The rat.

Until one hundred feet further . . . another skidding stop. The rat.

And then there were three.

# HORSE

When we were kids at this school,
we were famous for this,
me and Pauly.
We stunk the joint out
every time we took to the court,
and in spite of that,
we took to the court
every chance we got.
Crowds would gather.
We'd go an hour
without either of us sinking a shot.
Still all true.
*Clang*, my shot goes off the rim.
Points were never the point
of shooting.

*Clang.*

'Tsamatter with you? Pauly.

Pauly knows, because he knows me,

and he knows *stuff*,

and he knows the world,

and he has this keen perception thing going,

the way maniac people do.

He's not nuts, however.

But I don't want him to know.

Nothing, I tell him.

I lie because I'm afraid he might help.

The Lilly is the death flower did you know that,
    Oakley?

It is Saturday morning,

sun shining,

air biting

in a nice

October morning kind of a way,

and we are shooting

baskets in the school yard

of Edna St. Vincent Millay

Middle School,

which we attended as kids.

Vince,

we called it then and now.

Lilly's the death flower, well, yes,

I suppose I did know that. That is,
I knew the lilly showed up at funerals a lot.
I walk behind the basket, and attempt a shot
right over the backboard.
It's a game of horse.
A twelve-year-long
game of horse.
I think we're on
the letter O. Possibly I have an R.
Ever seen one of them? he asks.
Those funerals where they're all
deadly dramatic
and put a lilly flower
in the dead guy's
hands?
Ever seen one of them?
He is not within range of the basket.
He has to throw the ball
like a football for it to even come close.
He does,
and it doesn't.
You went out without me, he says,
watching me retrieve and square
up for another shot.
His hands are on his hips, and he walks
toward me without any sense

of purpose at all.

Defense is not really an issue with us.

You know I hate that, when you go out without
     me.

I know you do, I say, and throw the ball

clean over the backboard.

And still, you do it anyway, he says,

in such a sincere voice

I could laugh or bow my head

in shame.

As a compromise

I bow my head

and laugh.

Unamused,

arms akimbo,

he lets me chase

my own miss.

I pick up the ball, rest it on my hip,

and look back across to where my friend waits.

He stares at me,

I stare at him.

I sit on the curb.

He sits on the court.

Time

out.

To think about what I've done.

Or to think about what I haven't.
This is what he wants. My all.
Because that is what he donates. His all.


Time out.
I don't need a lot.
I get back up and walk over.
No Pauly, I say, I have never seen one of those
     funerals
deadly dramatic
where they place in lilly-white hands
a bone-white lilly.
And neither have you.
Okay I haven't, he says, but I have thought
     plenty
about being
buried with Lilly.
Christ Pauly,
is all I say
and all I should have to say.
Even he should know.


We have set up about ten feet apart, and are
     just passing the
ball back and forth,
first easy, gradually with more pepper.

Like, you want to be buried alive with her,
or will one of you be dead
and the other one's supposed to just
jump in?
He sighs, whips me the ball.
Oh, I don't know, he says. Just more
the *spirit*
of the idea that I like,
more than the
practical side of it.
Know what I mean?
Well, I whip it back, and tell him I do. He truly
    can't see
life post-Lilly.
But I still don't think the answer
is Lilly post-life.
There is no practical side, Pauly.
Pauly withdraws, backs away,
stretches his hands out toward the sky.
He wants the ball.
I pull back and heave it.
Passing, we do fine.
We are excellent passers.
He gathers it in, does his one well-rehearsed
    move,
a quick three steps

and two dribbles east-west across the lane,
and up goes his hook shot.
Doesn't hit the net,
the rim,
the backboard.
If it were possible to miss the ground,
that shot would have.
Pauly looks at me and I look at him and I smile my
good-bye.
I don't see why people have to leave, he says.
We don't need that, you and me.
It's like the whole world
happens to us right here, doesn't it?
I catch the hard throw and I throw the hard
    throw
and he throws again harder still.
I ratchet up.
He ratchets up and up again.

I don't want to throw the ball this hard
    anymore.
It is stinging my hands,
and the last one very nearly broke
through my grip and bashed me
in the face.

But I keep on, pushing up the speed.

I don't know, Paul. Maybe it's not such a bad
    thing,

even if it means friends,

and well, *friends*,

gotta split.

What is a friend for, after

all?

Is it to make the bad parts of life

feel a little better

by smoothing them over?

Or is it to help a person through

the truth

as painlessly as possible

while still

allowing it to be

the truth?

I want my friend to feel better,

not worse.

So why do I throw the ball as hard as I possibly
    can?

He laughs as he catches it, and

whips it back, harder.

I rear back, more like a pitcher than a
    basketball player.

*     *     *

As soon as it leaves my hand I know
this is it, this is the one, this is the break-through
ball that he cannot catch, and it is deadly
    face-high
and I don't know why I did it
and I want to pull it back.
I can even feel my body language,
the way you do that when you throw something
but you still need to control it as it flies.
I'm pulling it,
then steering it,
past his head one way,
then the other then over
his head, but it will not listen
and I am sick.
As Pauly drops his hands to his sides.
Not even attempting
to catch it.
Ducking it instead, at the last instant.
*Ping*, *ping*, and *ping* over again
as the ball bounces off away
beyond Pauly.
I must have my face all screwed up, because he
    is there,
squatting on his haunches, laughing.

* * *

He stands, runs down the ball, and returns.

He smiles.

Checks his watch.

Gotta go, kid.

Got a date.

He acts like this is not important.

I can't allow it.

I'm happy for you, Paul, I say calmly.

Happy for me?

How 'bout, for a change

you be happy for you?

He smiles more intensely,

like to show me the way,

of happy.

Happy you be,

light you see,

when finally

Oakley makes three.

Pauly likes rhyme. Good for Pauly.

No, thank you, I say more calmly,

but not a lot more calmly.

You want Lilly, he says. Bounces the ball once.

No, I want the ball. Give me the ball.

You want me, he says happily. Bounces the ball
    once.

I want the ball.

And Oakley makes three.

No. I just

want

the ball. Paul.

Give

me

the ball

Paul.

It's my shot.

# JUST TALKIN'

I'M NOT MY BROTHER'S KEEPER, I have to keep reminding myself. I'm barely my own.

"I am so psyched," Pauly says.

"Cool," I say.

"Psyched," he repeats. He keeps chattering his teeth together on purpose, making a castanet sound. But he repeatedly nods, nods at me, trying to force the same kind of enthusiasm out of both of us. As he speaks, as we ride in the open air in the bed of his truck, while Lilly drives alone in the cab, Pauly is holding my hand, and I am holding his.

I do my part. "Psyched."

There is a pause. There is reality. I can read by the ripples spanning his forehead that my "psyched" sounded as unconvincing to him as it did to me.

"I hope I don't blow it, Oakley. I hope I don't

muck this up altogether. I can do that—as you well know. I can make a royal shit-hole mess out of things if I really try."

I hate to hear him talking like this. I mean, it is true enough. But I wonder if it might be less true if he wasn't all the time suspicious of feeling good. "Stop it, Pauly. You're not gonna blow—"

"You know me, Oak."

And I hate it when he shifts it onto me. "No I don't."

"Come on, don't say that. You know me. You're the one, the smart one, the clever one. The inside one. You gotta know me. Nobody else knows me. So if then you don't know me it's like, I don't exist. Don't scare me, Oak."

"I know you, Pauly. And I won't scare you."

"Excellent. So tell me then why I do what I do so I can stop doing it."

"What did you do now, Paul?"

He just shakes his head, squeezes my hand. He is awfully awfully strong, my Paul. "Just tell me the why bit, Oak, huh?"

"I don't know why, Pauly. That's like a pyramids-of-Egypt question. Nobody knows where your thoughts come from, we all just stand back and go *wow*."

He likes that for a minute. Then he goes all quiet again. You know how, in roulette, you just keep waiting, and waiting for the wheel to come to a stop but it seems to just keep ticking off new numbers interminably . . . that's what it can be like, on certain days, waiting for the defining Pauly moment.

"This is the one, Oak. Today's the day. This is it, you know."

"Is it?"

"It is."

Lilly opens the small sliding window behind her head. "Do I know where I'm driving, or am I just, driving?"

Pauly doesn't seem to have heard. He's staring at the flying-by pine trees so intently, it's as if he's trying to count them all.

"Just driving, I guess, Lil," I say. "But it doesn't matter, because this is *it*. Today is the day. *It*."

"Is it?" she asks brightly. "Is it *it* again today? Funny, the radio didn't say anything about *it* this morning."

Pauly's back in the conversation, and mad, which is fair. Then, he's laughing, which is awfully good of him. "All right you guys, go on and zoo me. You'll be crying though, when I hit one of these times. Maybe when you try and come see me after I've made it, I won't even have security open the gate to let you in."

We all know what we're doing, we just don't know, except for Pauly, where. He got a painting gig for the two of us, through his uncle who is as of this month in the house restoration business. Next month he'll be in the wholesale fish and sweat socks business, and probably so will we.

Pauly is a huge student of Uncle Dizzy's wheeler-dealerism. Every time we get near the guy, fame and fortune are close at hand.

And Lilly is driving us for the simple but not so simple reason that Pauly likes to ask things of her. And Lilly likes to tell him yes.

"Come up here in the cab with me, you guys. I'm getting lonely."

"Too crowded," Pauly says.

"You could fit six of us up here, *and* a six-point buck." She has to yell to be heard, as she faces the road ahead and talks to the boys behind her.

"I am getting kind of cold, Paul," I say.

"You can go," he answers. "I don't mind. I like the wind on me, though, so I'm gonna stay for now. I don't feel cold, Oak. Really, cold doesn't bother me."

Pauly has never ever been sick in all the time I've known him, and I've known him as long as I've known me. I, on the other hand, catch every damn thing. He says I get sick for both of us. So he stays in the bed and I stay in the bed with him, and Lilly is a sport about doing the Dodge Ram chauffeur thing. And though he has given her no further instructions, she knows when she finds the house.

"Holy hell," Lilly blurts.

How to describe it? Ramshackle, for a start. Slanted, for another. Porches sloping off the place. Scalloped and gabled, waterlogged clap-board which was last painted back when that shade of . . . red, I think . . . was one of the four colors available down at the general store. On the two sides of the house that you can see from the long driveway approach, I count twenty-two windows. There are maybe three that are the same, standard size, with the rest being a collection of elongations, octagons, oval portholes, and stained-glass peekaboos.

There is a crew of five already setting up, dragging out drop cloths to protect the wild mad foliage close to the house, pulling ladders and tool buckets off the oversize pickup belonging to Diz. Lilly has stopped the truck a dozen yards short of the driveway's end, and is staring.

"*If* the ladders don't tip the place right over, it'll take you three months to paint this house."

Pauly laughs. Not angry or mocking, but excited. Myself, I'm already hoping the ladders do tip the joint over. He turns to Lilly hopefully. "Don't you think it's really something though, Lil? I couldn't wait for you to see it."

"Now I have. Pauly, come home," Lilly says sadly, as if the condition of the house somehow reflects badly on him. "You don't need this."

Paul hops over the side of the truck like a cowboy entering the corral. Lilly looks through the window at me. We exchange facial shrugs. Why should it be that one guy's daffy enthusiasm should be able to overwhelm another guy's solid common sense? I don't know either, but it keeps happening. Maybe it's the slugger theory, that even though he's struck out twenty times in a row he still keeps swinging so hard he's *got* to hit one a country mile. He's got to, right? I hop over the side of the truck after him.

Paul goes up to the driver's window. From behind I can read his whole body, stretching, lengthening, striving, as he reaches himself in that window to kiss Lil. I'm staring, I know I'm staring, at the back of his head. Staring, so badly, I know, I know.

A guy can love Lilly just by watching her love someone else.

"See ya, Oak," she says, as Paul pulls away from her and hurls himself toward the task at hand. "See ya then," she repeats when, apparently, I haven't received it all. And she points, at the back of our boy.

Despite my slowness, I do understand. We understand. You can't take an eye off him at a construction site, or near a cliff or a raging river. Or at a falling-down house where nobody's living and he has access to ladders and tools and stuff.

So sure, I understand. It's my shift.

"Pauly-o," Uncle Diz yelps as we approach.

"Dizzy!" Paul hollers back.

This much is true right out of the chute: The rest of the crew doesn't care for Pauly one bit. It takes a while to get to appreciate Pauly under the best of circumstances, and nobody here appears to have the time for it. For his part, Pauly appears not to notice.

"Yo boys," he says to the lot of them.

The lot of them fail to respond. They go on

hoisting ladders, dropping drop cloths, dumping tool buckets.

We are late, too. We need to catch up. "What do you want us doing, Dizzy?" I ask.

"I want you to come and get coffee and donuts with me."

"Maybe we should paint a little something first," Pauly says. "I wanna work, Unc. I wanna show you what I can do, and work my way up through the ranks, so I can take over your job. But I figure it all starts right here, with the paint and the ladders and stuff."

Dizzy makes a show of looking at himself. He is wearing designer jeans. Creased. And a black cashmere sweater. "Why would you want to start *there*? Cheese, I know what you can do, kid. Come on with me."

Pauly looks at me and shrugs. He is full of mad energy and a desire to throw himself at the job, but he's positively dying to get under his uncle's wing. I nod, telling him it's all right, and this sets him free. The two of them turn toward Dizzy's Lincoln Town Car without saying anything else directly to me.

The doors slam on the big boat Lincoln, and the wheels seem to start spinning the instant the engine cranks. They're kicking up gravel and dust as Dizzy fishtails left then right toward Dunkin' Donuts. I can hear the engine whine away in the distance as I stand there staring at the still-settling flume of driveway dirt.

I don't know a single person on the crew. I

don't know a thing about paint, or scrapers or ladders or drop cloths. I turn away from the vision of the rest of the world and focus on the proposed job at hand. I stare up and down. Attempt eye contact with each worker who crosses my line of vision, staring harder, looking dumber, craning my neck more with each very obvious snubbing of me. Nope, I won't be making a bunch of new friends today.

I can stare up at the house, though. Magnificent mess that it is. Sagging sloping Victorian whatsit with a madly steep-pitched roof, porches curling around everyplace, gables popping up all over like gophers from the ground. Silver maples on three sides hang close enough and touch the house in enough places that it looks like they're doing the job of holding the joint up, rather than actually helping to bring it down.

I am aware of staring. Not particularly concerned, but aware. I must appear to be either a potential buyer in the first browsy stages of shopping or one of those end-of-the-rope fog-eyed lunatics come back to chat up the old childhood homestead.

The whine of the car, reverse order. Getting stronger, cornering into the driveway, kicking up more rocks as the blacktop turns to dirt. All heads turn now, mine included.

The Lincoln stops about ten feet before me.

Pauly emerges, walks purposefully toward me. He takes me by the hand. Second time today, he's taking me by the hand.

"Right," I say quietly as he pulls me into the car. "You're gonna close me outside the mansion gate when you get rich, but you can't even make one trip to the coffee shop without me."

I am expecting a snappy retort. Instead he treats it like a real conversation.

"I was never really gonna lock you out." He gives the hand a squeeze.


Dunkin' Donuts. Dunkies, to players like us. Pauly and Dizzy are yakking up a storm, scheming, planning, concocting get-rich-quick schemes. Get *richer* quick I suppose it is for Dizzy. Get *anything* for Pauly.

I can't get in there with them. I like money fine, at least I like it a lot better than having none. It's the scheming, the planning and the concocting part that I just don't seem to be able to warm up to. That's one of the million and five ways Pauly and me are opposite. I honestly don't think Pauly cares at all whether he ends up with a dime when it's over or not, but the plotting and trickster stuff? He could live there and be happy, or something like happy anyhow. We could make a perfect team, with him conniving his way to wealth, then giving it all to me.

And the thing is, I think he would.

Dizzy, though, apparently likes both ends of that particular stick, the *having* of money and the grubby *acquiring* of it.

"You with me, Pauly?" Diz keeps saying. "You with me on this?"

Pauly is with him. Nodding madly. Speech-less with grubby desire.

Diz reaches across the table and shoves a twenty into my hand. "Do us a favor, kid, get ten large coffees, black. And a dozen donuts, mix 'em up."

I stare at the twenty. Okay then, so I'm not invited.

They really are a good work crew, I must say. Seems like half the house has been completely scraped down by the time we return. The dusty barn-red paint that was once clinging desperately to spongy clapboards is now coating the ground all around the house like a carpet, like a snow flurry in hell. The natural color of the wood sid-ing, streaked with the red, looks almost better than a full coat of paint would. But there is a lot of rot.

"Gonna take a lot of work, replacing so many clapboards," I say to nobody in particular as I hand out the coffees.

Various disgusted splutters of laughter come back to me from the crew.

"Where'd you get this rube, Pauly?" Dizzy asks, and claps me fondly on the back. "I buy 'em to sell 'em, kid. I'm not interested in making the thing livable, just sellable. I don't worry what's *under* the paint."

I look to Pauly, who's got that look on his face like he's busy taking mental notes. The wrong notes, I fear.

We haven't done much more than look the place over, shift tools and ladders from one spot to another, and listen to Dizzy wisdom by the time the boss declares lunch break. It is obvious now we are here mainly to be his audience. Again he wants us to go with him, but this time we're staying.

Pauly follows his uncle to the car. "I really want to show you, Dizzy, what I got. So what I figure is I'll be your foreman while you're away," Pauly says. "Making sure everything's proceeding—being like, you, in your absence. So why don't you gimme the phone, the keys to the house . . . and these shades." He reaches out and takes the sunglasses, which are hanging on a chain around Dizzy's neck. Dizzy gives it all up good-naturedly.

"Okay," he says, "go on and show me then."

As Dizzy roars away in the car, the crew silently goes back to business. It is like Pauly and I are not even there. We head for the front door. Pauly puts on the glasses and starts dialing the phone with his thumb, like a pro. He's got his other arm slung like an anaconda across my shoulders.

He refuses to remove his arm from me as he unlocks the door. So I kind of lurch forward and down, as his key hand pulls close to the cracking oak door. Forehead to the big beveled window that takes up a third of the door, I see me right up close.

Furrowed brow and squinted eyes, the

Oakley I see doesn't know who he's seeing.

It's quite a maneuver for me to twist up and get a look at Pauly, but I do it, managing not to disturb the grip he's got on me because when they happen those grips mean something and breaking them too would sure as hell mean something.

I'm looking up at my man Paul, in the stupid opaque shades, with the phone in his ear and the key in the door, his friend—his only friend, but you didn't hear it from me—under his arm and a key in the door of a place he's got no business going into. And a smile of smile of smiles slashed across his face.

"I'm gonna *make* it happen, Oakley," he says, and he is simultaneously killer serious and near giddy with joy. "Dizzy's gonna make me his partner when he sees what I can do. This is my big chance. This house is gonna be *finished* when he gets back from lunch."

I try to rewind.

"What, exactly, is going to be finished, Pauly?"

He's now paying closer attention to the phone than to me. "Why doesn't she answer?" he asks.

"Why don't *you* answer?" I ask.

"What?"

"What is going to be finished by the end of lunch? The front of the house? The prep work? What?"

Please, I'm thinking, let him give me the right

answer. Please, I pray, though I do not pray unless absolutely necessary.

The key will not move in the door. No worry. No hurry.

"My house," he says, smiling, confident. "That really is a good crew out there. You see those guys bustin' tail, Oakley?"

It may very well be, I realize, that the reason I don't seem to be able to invest my heart in much of anything is that I fight it, and him, and myself. I am equal parts excited by the possibility and convinced of the old futility. "Oh Pauly," I say. "Pauly, that can't—"

"So while those guys are getting the outside done, and I'll be pushing them really hard . . . you can be in here and you'll do the first floor and I'll take the second floor . . ."

If it were a matter of spirit. If you could make things happen by *want*, then Pauly's vision would come true. But if things were simply that, then much would come true for Paul. But, not much does.

"Pauly," I say. "Pauly, that can't happen. That is not humanly possible. . . . Nobody could expect that of you, and I think you'd probably die in the attempt. And maybe I'm being a little selfish, but I'd rather let your dream die and keep you."

His smile is warm and benevolent and I have this fleeting moment when I think I see on his face that he appreciates, realizes . . . But I'm just wishing it.

"And as much as I love you, Oakley, *that*, I gotta tell you, is why you're never gonna get anywhere. Thinkin' like that."

He hangs up the flip on the phone, lets go of me, and works harder on the dry uncooperative lock.

Pauly rattles the door and shakes it, wiggles the knob, and finally kicks the green tarnished brass plate at the foot. Kicks it again, pissed, works the key until I am sure it will break, or that Pauly will, then finally we are in the foyer.

"Nice fuckin' foyer," he says. "Welcome home. Doesn't it say welcome the hell home, Oak? It sure does, and it's beautiful."

And it is. Red and blue and green threadbare but stylish oriental rug. Dark wood paneling and a brass gas lamp–style light sticking out of one wall. It's a warm-feeling place, like a rich person's library.

Pauly's hit the redial already.

"Why won't she answer? Where is she? She doesn't have anything doing today. I asked her and she said she doesn't have anything doing today."

"So? So she *got* something doing, what's the big deal, Paul?" But at the same time, I want him to keep dialing till he gets her.

"In my truck. In my truck, she got something doing? She better not be up to the old tricks. Not in my truck anyway."

Pauly snaps the phone closed again.

"She never had any old tricks, for one thing.

And it's not even your truck for another." It's more of a long-term loaner, since Pauly's father skipped out and just sort of forgot to take his wheels with him.

"Ya . . . well . . . just the same. She starts that stuff, I swear I'll just . . . When I see her this time, I'll just . . ."

He can't even finish it. Not as a threat, not as a bluff, not as a joke. I know it, he knows it, and the creaky steps we climb in the beautiful old house know it. So I help him out.

"You'll just . . . fall on your knees and rub her feet? Or, you'll just . . . buy her a box of chocolates and take her to a movie?"

Pause. He'd like to do better than that. If there were any other witnesses he might.

"Ya, something like that," he says, then laughs. "But that would sure teach her a lesson wouldn't it, Oak? She'd never mess with ol' Pauly again, would she?"

"No," I say, following him to the top of the stairs and into the first bedroom. "No, Pauly, I don't suppose she would."

He plunks himself down on an old bed so springy it bounces another six times before settling down. Like a car with bad shocks. He's dialed again. Outside the window we can hear the rattling, scraping, clamoring of the crew attacking the house. They appear to be responding well to Pauly's style of leadership.

As he waits for the phone, he points out the window. "See?" he says, and winks.

"Just . . . we might fall a little short of your goal, Pauly, so don't get . . . too rigid about it. We'll do our best. . . ." I do not want to point out that, on top of all the other difficulties in getting a three-week job done in an hour and a half, he and I aren't actually *doing* anything still. Somewhere in there, he sees different.

He hangs up the phone. Sighs hard like a little boy denied a trip to the candy store. Stomps past me wordlessly, bumping me deliberately on his way by. But that's okay.

We poke our heads into each of the other three bedrooms, similar cozy but shabbified bedrooms. Somebody else's bedrooms. The last one, at the end of the hall, the corner room, with windows on two sides, that is the one Pauly names his bedroom.

"Yup," he says, bouncing on the bed. He dials.

I leave him and go exploring down the narrow yellow-walled rear staircase. Wind up in the grease-stained yellow kitchen. I would never eat in this kitchen. I would never eat anything that had been prepared in this kitchen. I wouldn't shake hands with anyone who had eaten in this kitchen. It looks almost as if there was a fire, and the people of this house had to flee in the middle of a meal. Two years ago. Crumbs and smears and drops of stuff—unfathomable stuff, after all this time—spill out of boxes in open cupboards, off plates at a perfectly set table, and cover the countertops, stove, and floor. The refrigerator, which I wouldn't open on a bet, is the fat old-style Frigidaire. The stove is a gigantic iron thing with two huge ovens suitable for cooking a whole entire person, if that's what you're into. The chairs and table are thick solid oaky things, dark-oiled and heavy-looking. Goofy cartoony curtains hang at the windows, with cats chasing butterflies all over them. All the shelves and drawers are covered in shiny orange shelf paper. You could write your name in the thick grease that covers every bit of wall, and the entire place is a mouse-turd plantation.

It is a great room. If I were a painter I would paint this room. Not that kind of painting the room, the kind I'm actually here to do and which I am not doing, but the other kind of painting, the kind artists do. This is a room for that. It *talks*, this room does.

I am about to explore further when I hear Pauly in the room above me. He's talking, but then not. You can hear pretty well through these walls and floors.

I quick-step it back up the stairs and round right back into the room where I left him.

He's talking on the phone. He's talking, lying on his back, rolling side to side.

"It's it," he says, the pitch of his voice climbing out of his real range. "It's it, Lilly, it's *the* it. This is the score . . . my uncle and me . . . he's going to let me in all the way once I prove myself. The whole real estate thing, we're gonna do it together, the buying and selling and rehabbing . . .

and I got, for you, a huge huge surprise. . . ."

He's still got the sunglasses on. He's got his free hand on his head as if he cannot believe his great fortune. He's writhing there on the bed.

"So call, huh, when you get this message. Wanna talk to you, Lil, wanna talk to you, sweetie. . . ."

I don't know if it's not apparent to Paul what was apparent to me, or if it simply does not matter to him. We go on. BAU, as he likes to say. Business As Usual. That's a Pauly joke, see. We wouldn't recognize *usual* if it flew up our noses.

"I love this house," Pauly says. "This house is gonna be my house, Oakley. How you fuckin' like that? It's gonna be *mine*, can you believe it? Then I'm gonna, after it's mine, gonna give it to Lilly."

I'm listening. Wishing and hoping and all that, but mostly listening. And smiling and nodding.

"Big house. Big enough, way," Pauly says. "You wanna live here with us, Oak? You can, y'know. Like, rent free. What am I saying, of course ya do. Just help me here and there with the fixin' up. You shouldn't wanna live in that divey place above the coffee crap place anymore. You live with me. Lilly and me and you. Fuckin' ay, Oak, huh?"

I have to remind myself that I am supposed to be the level-headed one. That this scheme should hold nothing but terror for me. That the idea should be not only impractical but deeply unsettling.

Yet for an instant I get none of that, and instead feel a warm shot of something through my belly.

I wait a couple beats. I know these moments too well. I pull it back, must speak carefully. "It is, Pauly. It is a great house. So, then, your uncle's gonna make it possible . . . ?"

"We're workin' on it. Shit's gonna happen. But it's a go, man, it's a go. We got it all figured up."

I nod, as it is the only strategy I can muster. "But Lilly's . . . Remember, Paul? Once the school year's up—"

He raises a hand to shut me up which is fine since I got further than I had expected to.

"That's just because—okay?—because she doesn't know the possibilities. She thinks about dead ends in Whitechurch but I think about the opportunities. She is really kind of limited that way, so I'm doing the figuring for us. To make it possible for her to be happy *here*, Oakley, see? I know she really wants to be happy *here*—"

The phone rings, and he is all smiles answering it.

"Ya, sweetie, ya. Big stuff. But I'll fill you in more in person. Oh, unbelievable. No, no you gotta wait. But here's a hint—don't go packing your bags for Boston just yet. . . ."

I am listening, I am picturing Lilly's expression.

"Ya. Well, ya, he's here, but so what? This is our moment, Lilly . . . no, no, he just left. Never mind. I'll talk to ya later."

He sits there on the bed, staring at the phone.

"Did she want to talk to me?" I ask.

"No," he snaps. "Where did you go, anyway?"

"Kitchen," I say.

"How is it then?" he asks.

"Needs work."

"Let's see."

So we do, down the yellow stairs to the needy old kitchen. Pauly stands there in the middle of it, and I still can't tell exactly what he thinks because the glasses are obscuring the windows to his soul. But he does this arms-spread, taking-it-all-in, *Sound of Music* twirl, sizing up every inch of the room. Then he stops still.

"This is it," he says. "This is where I am needed most. Change of plans. You take the upstairs. I am going to save the life of this house, right here in the heart." He rolls up his sleeves, like for surgery.

I shake my head. "Jesus, Paul, this is an awful lot of work. . . ."

He finds a loose sheet of wallpaper in one corner, starts clawing it down. "We are not afraid of work," he insists. "Come on, Oakley, are we afraid of work?"

"Well, I suppose it's not the work, exactly—"

"Good," he says, "good man. Let's kick some ass, Oak, me and you." He whips around now and—it does not matter whether he has the glasses on or not—I can see in the windows. "We can do it, I am certain we can do it, Oakley, if you're behind me. You're behind me, right? Right, we'll show him. Then we'll show her . . . she can't be doubting, y'know, Oak, or nothing works, right, y'know?"

There is no answer. There is no answer that will say what I want to say to Pauly without saying what I do not want to say. So the two of us spend ten ridiculous minutes circling the room, pulling down a strip of wallpaper here, pulling up a strip of linoleum there. I am near despairing when help, or at least diversion, arrives.

"Pauly," Lilly says from the doorway of the kitchen. She is looking all around, and where Paul sees potential, she . . . fails to see potential.

We look at each other, me and Lilly. We don't know why she's here. We are very glad she is.

"The more I thought about it . . . you don't need this crap work, Paul . . . come on home."

He is flabbergasted. "What are you doing here? I didn't tell you to come . . . you're ruining everything . . ."

"Let's get out of here, Paul—"

"Fuck, Lilly. I'm onto something huge here. I told you that. What are you—" He stops himself, very quickly stares into me—rips off the sunglasses to do it—then at her. "Sonsobitches," he says low, then puts the sunglasses back on. "You're wrong. This time you're wrong."

"Pauly," she says, sympathetically, which is her mistake.

"Just shut up," he says, then leads her out. "C'mon, I'll drive you home. You can lie on the floor if you're too embarrassed to be seen with me."

He is making tracks, and she rushes to keep up. Uninvited, I follow.

It's a pretty silent ride, and I can feel Pauly pulling away from us. Down down down the old hill we go until he kicks her—and me, go figure—out of his truck which isn't even his, right outside the church. She tries to speak, but he pays no attention.

"What the hell?" is all Lilly can say as we stand there watching the pickup tear down the street.

"He's convinced this time." I shrug.

"I almost wish he wouldn't even try. . . ."

The sound of that bottoms me out so badly, I can't muster the muscles to shrug. Then the two of us, Lilly and me, me and Lilly, which I normally love to hear myself think in either direction but now feels so fractured, we sit right there on the curb waiting for the inevitable. "Inevitable," it occurs to me, is a good word for events in Whitechurch.

It takes roughly ninety seconds to drive the length of Main Street, turn left, come up the same length of Middle Street, and wind up back here at the church.

"He thinks he's really got it for sure this time, huh, Oakley?"

"He thinks so. I don't know what Dizzy told him, but Pauly's long-gone sold."

Lilly leans into me with her shoulder, and

ever so ever so slightly I let the weight of me fall into her. "Ah, Oakley," she says, and she sounds exhausted.

"Ya," I say.

It's been just about ninety seconds.

He pulls to the curb. No, he creeps to the curb. Rolls down the window.

"You gotta baby-sit tonight?" Lonely, he asks.

She nods.

"Can't I, you think, this once?"

She shakes her head.

"Oh, go on, ask him. Whatsit hurt?"

"The Rev hates your guts, Pauly. There's no way."

He looks at me, looks and sounds genuinely angry with me. "Get your shoulder off my girl-friend."

I don't.

"See me later, then," Pauly says. Strong. A statement.

Lilly waits. Not a flutter.

"See me later, then?" Pauly asks. Soft. A request. More than a request, really.

"Sure," she says. "Love to."

He is so excited, smiling goofy like a child. Also like a child, he seems like maybe he shouldn't be allowed to drive a truck. He races the engine, accidentally lets it roll. Puts it in reverse to return to the conversation. Gone, he is, off to Lovelillyland. Like she has said yes for the first time right here right now instead of right here four years ago. Gone, like he is every time. First time every time.

"I'll come get you here, at nine then, is it?"

"Nine it is." Lilly stands. She is smiling, no longer tired. She has made Pauly happy, or whatever it is Pauly gets when the rest of us would get happy. All she wanted to do in the first place. All right now. All nice.

"And you, bird-dog girlfriend-stealing skinny bastard. Get in the truck. I'm gonna take you someplace secluded. Kick yo' ass. Teach ya not to be messin' with my old lady."

I stand, look slowly up, then slowly down, the street. I brush off the seat of my pants. "Might as well, I guess. Nothin' else doing around here around now. Kick my ass, then we'll get back to work."

He's up again, Power Pauly. I love to see him this way. And I worry.

"First, lemme buy you a Coke. And while we're drinkin' I'm gonna lay out the Plan."

"We got time?" I ask.

"Get in the truck," he says.

I climb in the truck.

Then he's buying me the Coke, at the fountain at the counter in the drugstore where they still have fountain drinks. I realize in lots of places this just isn't so anymore, but Whitechurch simply couldn't be, without the drugstore with the fountain where you can get a vanilla or cherry Coke and it may be too flat and so syrupy you're happy you're drinking in a place that also sells

mouthwash, toothpaste, and floss. The cell phone
rings but Pauly ignores it. He's talk talk talking,
about the Plan, which I thought would be about
high finance and real estate, but turns out to be
about a potbellied stove and exposed beams and
parquet flooring. The kitchen. His kitchen. And
nothing but the kitchen. He's ignoring the phone,
which keeps ringing, and the looks from customers and Willomena who works the fountain
when her mother is around to watch the kids.

"It's just gonna be for Dizzy. He should have
a service for that. I got more important things to
do with my time. He brought me in to come up
with killer ideas and imagination, like I'm doing
right now. A hot knife through butter, I'm gonna
be in this organization."

The more important things amount to talking. This Pauly can do with the best of them. He's
talking, right, about what he's going to do with
that house when he gets it, and what he's going
to do in and around that house when it's just
right, and which bedroom is going to be mine
and the hundred and fifty million thousand
things he can do in that house to make Lilly
happy. But in Pauly's view it all—the house, the
business, the future, everything—revolves around
the masterpiece that will be that kitchen. Lilly
would die for a kitchen like that, he says.

"You know, Oak," Pauly says, and I can see
the sincere dripping out of the corners of his eyes,
sunglasses or no sunglasses, "I love to make her
happy."

And like, what the hell. How could you ever tell him the truth?

The phone rings again.

"Pauly, what if it's not *for* Dizzy? What if it *is* Dizzy?"

It's my own fault, but he pops off one of his awful instapoems, which he thinks are okay because he figures you get extra points for on-the-spotness, but I figure you don't.

### Dizzy #1

When opportunity rings

you best take what it brings

Don't try to guess what is

cause it might look

like

Diz


It rings on, whether it is opportunity, Dizzy, or any combination thereof.

"Willow," Pauly calls, and she slides on over to us. "Willow, honey it's for you."

She takes the phone. "It's for me? Nobody ever calls for me. Damn."

I wish he would just play this one straight. "Cut it out Pauly, take the call."

"What? What? I can't hardly understand you," she says, wincing at the phone, pulling back and looking at it as if to understand it better. "Ya, he's here. Where is here? Well here is the drugstore of course, where'd ya think? Hello? Hello?"

She hands Pauly back the phone.

"Was it Dizzy?" I ask, because Pauly is not concerned enough to do it. If he would only be concerned enough . . . so many times, so little effort, would save him so much trouble.

"Two more Cokes please, Miss Willomena?" Paul asks.

"Yes," she says to Paul, then, "Yes," to me. "I believe that's who he said he was. And he said to keep your ass on that stool 'cause he's on the way over."

"Cool," Paul says. "Then make it three Cokes. We'll do a deal over a couple of cold ones right here."

"Ah, maybe I better go," I say. "You and your uncle might want to—"

"Still no stomach for the fast lane, huh?" Pauly says as I give up my stool.

Dizzy bursts in. He marches toward the counter so hard you can just about feel him pounding over the broad black-and-white tiles.

Pauly opens his arms.

Dizzy walks right up to him. Slaps him across the head. Not that hard, not punishing, but an attention-getter.

I grab Dizzy's arm and he turns a meaty dark glare on me that nearly makes me let go and run. I do neither, though. I look at Paul, with the glasses now hanging diagonally across his pale

soft face, one gray eye exposed in all its sad dis-
belief.

Willomena is placing two tall vase-shaped
glasses on the counter. She backs quickly away.

"I bought you a Coke," Paul whispers.

"I want to give you chances, Pauly," he says,
not unkindly but killer anyway, maybe because
of the not-unkindness. "But you just don't have
a thing, nothing on the ball. I put you in charge
for half a day, you disappear. You don't answer
the phone, book out of work, don't do one single
thing. Have I got it about right, Paul? Is this
pretty much what you accomplished today?"

I wish Dizzy had just silently beat him up
instead.

Pauly is nearly crying. "It's not like that, Diz.
I was working. I was doing some serious planning, designing, figuring. . . ." He picks up off the
counter a napkin on which he had been drawing
while talking to me. I was not even aware that
the talk and the drawing were related.

"Good, Paul," he says, "so you drank Coke
*and* doodled. Big day."

Dizzy reaches out and practically decapitates
his nephew with the chain as he takes back the
sunglasses. "I'm sorry," he says. "But, ah, no . . ."

Paul's still whispering. "Diz. My house—"

"Excuse me?"

"My house. You said we could work something. With the house. Do a deal. Then it would
be *my* house."

Dizzy grabs Pauly's face with his two hands and holds it there, talking slowly and directly into it. He is a surprisingly powerful man, but he holds Pauly's face with great gentleness, restraint.

"Pauly. Pauly. I was just talkin'. Don't you understand? Don't you know the difference? You're a talker yourself, right, so you should know. You're supposed to know the difference."

Pauly hands over the phone. Already Dizzy seems different, no longer all that angry, a little regretful. That's Pauly's life for you, right there.

"Pauly, Pauly, Pauly. You're just . . . dangerous, is what you are. You don't think like the rest of us think. You're a good kid with some nuts and bolts that just ain't tightened all the way up."

With his phone and his glasses and not another word, Dizzy heads out.

I expect drama. I expect now for Pauly to take a bite out of the Formica counter or remove his shoes and throw them through the plate-glass window. I think that's what I would do. And if he wants me to help him damage something that isn't himself, I believe I will.

But he quietly sits back down in front of his drink. I sit in front of the other. He takes a big slurpy-sound drink, then grins. He has a beautiful smile, Paul does.

"I've got your nuts and bolts right here, Dizzy," he says, jingling the keys to the house.

\* \* \*

When Lilly comes by at ten that night, I'm already ready to go.

"He never showed," she says, in a voice I know pretty well.

"Uh-huh," I say. "You up for a walk? Probably take us an hour."

She sighs, takes my hand.

The part I know is that we will find him in the house he thought would be his. And Lilly's. And mine. The part I worry about is what kind of antics he will be up to when we get there.

We find him in the kitchen. He's eating a bowl of cereal. He sees us come in and pours, as if we are right on time, two more bowls.

I pray that he has at least rinsed them out, because I *will* eat in this kitchen. The three of us eating in our kitchen.

# BIBLIOPHILIA

**M**OST PLACES I GO, I want them with me. Or anyway I want at least one of them with me. Like, at the movies, I want either one of them with me and I don't particularly care which one as long as it's not both because together they talk too much. At the schoolyard basketball court it's Pauly, and at loads of other places it's Lilly. It all makes its own kind of sense and we don't for the most part need to question it too much. But then sometimes we do. Sometimes we need a place apart.

The library is that place. The Whitechurch Library. If ever my friends cannot find me, that is where they search, and that is where they usually succeed in locating me. The way an old dog finds his way back over miles and miles to his home when somebody tries to shove him off on a farm someplace, that is how I find my way back to the library. It's my place, even more than my place is. Though I find myself spending less time here over time. As a kid I spent day and night in this building, warmed and entertained by it. Day, and night.

"You are so boring, Oakley, you're in a category all by yourself," Lilly teases as the two of them come ambling through the door.

"Good," I say. "So get out of my category."

"Come with us," Lilly says, taking my hand and pulling gently, playfully. "You don't even read. Why bother?"

But I don't want to play. "Am I bothering *you*?"

She's right, though. About the no reading. Didn't use to be. But is.

"As long as we're here," Pauly says, "why not let's look him up?"

I pay no attention as Paul trots off to get the dictionary and look me up. I am staring at Ophelia Lennon, the one and only librarian of the town of Whitechurch. There used to be two. She is tall, maybe five ten. And slim, with square shoulders that make her look like one fine column all the way to the floor, the line of her yellow-flowered brown dress unbroken by any hint of hip. All her dresses reach the floor, and that is part of the mystery of her—there could be anything under there. Her hair is in between brown and black, with generous splatters of gray all over. It is combed straight back to reveal a mighty forehead, and to rest in a gentle flip at the base of her neck. She moves deliberately, surely, but it seems she's going at a speed one tick slower than the rest of us, like the Disney heroines always do. Grace, is what it is. And she wears perfectly round rimless spectacles that are exactly the same size as her eye sockets, giving her pale, nearly white eyes the ghostly look of ancient Greek statuary—which the library features in miniature in every cranny and cove. She looks very much in fact like a statuette in nonfiction called *Aphrodite Victorious*. Maybe not the body, exactly, but their faces are very much alike.

"She looks like Buddy Holly," Lilly says. "You ever see pictures of him?"

"You know, Lilly," I snarl, "that's pretty sick, being opposed to books and libraries and librarians. Maybe you're a category too. Bibliophobia. Look her up while you're there, Pauly."

"Jealous?" Lilly laughs. But if I was wrong, she could do a lot better than that.

"Here it is," Pauly says, sitting down at our round oak table with a massive gold *Webster's Encyclopedic Unabridged Dictionary*.

"You're very proud of yourself for having taken only ten minutes to find a reference book in a one-room library," I say.

"Hey," he points out, "one *big* room."

"Here," Lilly says. "'Bore: To weary by dullness.'" She slams the big book shut, making a broad hollow thump that causes Ophelia Lennon to shoot us a look.

This upsets me. "Dammit, Lilly, now look.

Ophelia Lennon is angry."

"Stop wearying me with your dullness, will you, Oakley?" Lilly whispers.

I point a finger at Lilly's perfect pug nose. "You are just jealous."

"Of what?" Pauly wants to know, but doesn't really want to know. He makes like he's really caught up in the dictionary.

"I'll tell you what," Lilly says, giving me a shut-up stare that her boyfriend cannot see. "I'm jealous that, because of whatever Oakley's doing for the dusty old library lady, he gets to keep the last book he borrowed—like, ten years ago—without paying any fines."

"Cool," Pauly says. "Maybe I'll do it too."

"Right." I snort. "First, you never even took out a library book . . ."

"And second," Lilly adds, "you never—"

"That's enough," Pauly blurts, loudly.

Ophelia Lennon throws us a look, because my friends clash with the library's style. And they will get worse. The two of them save their poorest performances for the library. My library. I did better when I was five. When I was four.

"Beat it, will ya, guys," I say.

"Well, he might be able to please your lady friend, but beat it?" says Lilly.

"All right, that does it," Paul says, even louder now. He rises from his seat and starts unbuckling his pants. We all laugh—except Paul, of course—at the threat the whole town has heard before. "I'll show ya."

Even Ophelia Lennon laughs. She laughs like a songbird.

"She laughs like a donkey," Lilly says. She doesn't mean anything by it, really, she just forgets sometimes.

"Shut up, Lilly," I say. This is very, very not us. But none of us are us here. This building is not us. It is me. I understand Lilly, but I do not sympathize. "Shut up and go—I mean it."

"Sorry," she says. "Um, you're not coming with us, I take it."

"Catch you later," I say, and they go without a fight. Pauly never does show us.

I'm alone with Ophelia Lennon. Almost. There is Teddy in his U.S. Postal Service uniform, sleeping at the newspaper rack. But he really doesn't count. I'm alone with Ophelia Lennon.

Not that I really do much about it. I watch her restack books. I watch her make herself her regular four-fifteen cup of banana tea, then watch her dunk her anisette toast into it. I watch her dust and sweep the room because, as I said, she is responsible for everything about the Whitechurch Library. On days when Ophelia Lennon is sick, the library doesn't even open.

There is no need for me to pretend to be reading or researching or doing a single damn useful thing with my time. Because nobody is watching. Nobody is watching, as the winter wind bounces off the thin windowpanes, trying to get in. Teddy is there, but he's Dead Ted, and you couldn't wake him if you drove a semi through the room pulling on that honky air horn.

So nobody's watching me watching Ophelia Lennon move her body through her day. Except Ophelia Lennon. She's watching me watching, and it's all right with her and it's all right with me. Only if another somebody comes in does she make me get a magazine or something, so it all doesn't look weird.

Then there's nothing left. It's time to close up the library, and Ophelia Lennon does that. There's a power to it, the way this building, this quiet smart domain of hers, bends, gives to her. She has the keys to the doors, she turns the heat down. And she turns the lights off, one at a time, when it's five o'clock and very dark.

By the time we have to wake Teddy and get him out, there are only two dull lights burning from the vaulted ceiling of the old mahogany room, the two lights Ophelia Lennon keeps on when she leaves. The glow from those small yellow bulbs seems to come from nowhere when it lights you up. Seems to come, rather, from inside you, inside your skin. When I approach Teddy, the light seems to come from under his denim-blue flap-hat. When Teddy is up and toddling out and I'm turned back looking at Ophelia Lennon again, the light is burning up from under her collar.

"What?" she says, and tilts her head in a quizzical way that makes me worry what kind of look I'm giving her.

"I didn't say anything," I say.

Ophelia Lennon nods, then starts to gather up her stuff, her going-home ritual.

"Can I help with anything?" I ask. "Books to reshelve, windows to close . . ."

She sighs, comes close to me with her coat over her arm.

"People are going to start to talk," she says sweetly.

"Cool," I say in return.

"Well, no. Oakley, when are you going to stop doing this? Hmm? This is not a good thing. You once spent a great many wonderful hours here, and now you spend too many pointless ones. Do you remember that you could recite big bites of Wordsworth by the age of seven? Do you remember that? 'I wandered lonely as a cloud/That floats on high o'er vales and hills,/When all at once I saw a crowd,/A host, of golden daffodils.' Do you remember?"

It is out of respect that I let her finish, though it is the sound of a car wreck to my ears.

"And 'The Raven.'" Ophelia Lennon is swept up in something now, nostalgia or mania or whatever. But she comes up, intimate-close, and pokes me lightly in the chest. "Every word, by the time you were nine. Oakley, I was absolutely certain you were going to be a poet like your mother."

You are not supposed to say that, Ophelia Lennon. Didn't we understand, you and I, that you were not supposed to say that?

Absolutely short-circuited. My wires are so

frayed at this moment, I am powerless to keep from doing the most insane and inexplicable thing of my life. I lurch forward and try desperately to kiss Ophelia Lennon. And this move is so far from what she, or any other sentient being, would have expected, I almost pull it off.

For a moment she is confused—though not quite as much as I am. But she gets her hands up between us just in time.

"What could you be thinking?" She is a little angry, but less than she has a right to be. I've got no answer, but I don't think she really expected one. She shakes her head in wonder. "Listen, Oakley, I loved your mother more than anyone on this earth. Almost as much as you did, and that is a lot because I have still never seen anything in life to compare to the two of you. And it is one of the treasures of my existence, the memory of our days here in this place, the three of us . . . and I am warmed by the very thought of you. . . ."

"See," I say because, apparently, I have not yet completed my descent into madness.

"No, not 'see.' You give me a warm feeling, true enough. But so does *Doctor Zhivago*, and that has nothing to do with the realities of my life either. It is so clearly time for this to stop. I have watched you, and I have hoped for something else, something better, something bigger, something further, something different. So you will not be a poet. That is a pity, but not necessarily a tragedy. The troubling part is watching you pull inward, and backward. In time. In geography.

"Turn around, son. Go the other way. Please."

The daffodils poem sounds remotely familiar, but it is probably just one of those things like, "I took the road less traveled by," or "The mass of men lead lives of quiet desperation." You know, stuff everybody picks up by osmosis just because there are teachers and librarians and just general jerks spitting it out at you throughout your life. She is exaggerating me as a kid, Ophelia Lennon is, and the only reason I don't say she is outright lying is out of respect.

"I'm sorry," I say.

She takes my shoulders firmly and turns me toward the exit. We head out, and the last thing is, she pulls on and buttons up her red cloth coat with the faux fur collar against the wind that has been waiting out there to bite at me and Ophelia Lennon.

It is possible I remember that coat. I have another haywire urge, this time to bury my face in that collar, and to have the wearer wrap her arms around me. But it is a very very very different urge from the last urge. The opposite, in fact. I think, though, that I will get a grip in time. I will sort. But for now I'm thinking it will be enough to be near, near the coat and the wearer and the library.

I do reach out and touch the sleeve though. I rub rough cloth between my fingers and I know it. I know I know the feel of that coat. I close my eyes for seconds.

"Oakley," Ophelia Lennon says as the bitter wind tears over us. "I don't want you coming around here and wasting away like you have been. If you come into this library again, I want it to be to make use of the books. To make use of *you*. Otherwise, don't come." She turns up her collar for emphasis, for punctuation.

I wonder for a moment if I can do that, go back into the books in the Whitechurch Library.

"I'm sorry," I say. "For what I tried to do. I won't try it again, I swear."

"Don't apologize," she says. "I half think I'd let you, if it meant you'd read John Donne with me again."

I reach out and shake her hand.

"I'll see you around, Ophelia Lennon." I can feel my head shaking no. "But I'll be leaving you and John Donne be."

I turn around quickly because I cannot bear to read her face.

Older folks and their funky saddening memories. I simply don't have the strength.

# PLACE & TIME

Who do you love?
Why?
What do you do?
Where?
Home.
The place
where when you go
they have to let you in.
More
still more
poetic
gobbledygook.
Why,
and why

does the poet

lie?

Because he is Lucifer

and that's what the devil does?

Or because he is your friend

and that's what your friend does?

And is there a difference?

Or does the distinction

matter?

Lie.

Because life itself

is not truthworthy.

Hi Dad, I say

at home

to my father's head

or his back

on the couch.

Or Hi Dad, I say

at home

to his indentation

in the couch.

That is home.

And I'm one

of the lucky ones.

Your people are your home.

And they do not have to let you in

if they don't feel like it.
Whitechurch
is my home.
Sentenced
to Whitechurch
like the man says.
It is my place.
I know my place.
Place and time.
My place
is seven hills
and very few people
scattered among them.
Ever seen a mouse
try to escape
a bathtub?
My time
suspended.
Time.
Unlimited.
Unfortunately.
Time
so lightly
does its business
that nothing
seems to be happening.

Do I have a time?
Preacher says we do
all
have a time.
To be born
to die
to love
to hate
to everything
there's a season.
What do I do with my season,
with my time
when it gets here?
Do I dare disturb the universe?
A friend wanted to know.
But we have an agreement.
I won't disturb the universe
as long as the universe
doesn't
disturb
me.

# A Smile Relieves a Heart That Grieves

FUNNY PLACE, WHITECHURCH on Sunday mornings. Funny place most of the time, but on a Sunday morning after church is letting out it's a differently funny place than usual. Particularly considering that it's a town named after the very church almost everyone is piling out of. And added to that we still do black Sunday clothes here, so we can be a pretty scary lot, dark-clouding it up and down our streets.

We're on our way home from church. It happens a few times a year. It is Pauly's idea. It is never my idea to go to church. Not that I have anything against church. There is plenty to recommend it. It is the tallest building in town. And the pointiest. There is no spot in town where your eye isn't pulled to this brilliant white god rocket of a steeple, and you can't help thinking, Yes, something goes *on* there. Board this rocket, and you will go someplace.

It is a suggestive building, and maybe if services consisted of walking around and around and around it, then that might be the thing. But now and then I go inside and—no bang. I like the outside better.

Pauly believes there's more to it, but mostly what he does is fidget and stare up one wall and down another, sit and stand and kneel at all the wrong times, and appear basically lost. But game. Trying his ass off to pull something from it.

Anyway, we are on our way home from church.

"'Get thee behind me, Satan,'" sayeth Pauly.

This is what he does. Always comes away with some bit that caught his ear. No context, though. He has little interest in, or little capacity for, context.

"'Get thee behind me, Satan,'" he repeats. "I love the sound of that. Oak, don't you love the sound of that?"

"Ya, it's all right. Beats 'Do unto others,' I guess. Sometimes it seems like every time we come, it's 'Do unto others' week."

"Ah, what are you talking about? I like 'Do unto others.' 'Do unto others' is so . . . rich with possibilities. You don't know what you're talking about, Oakley. 'Do unto others' kicks ass. After 'My god, my god, why hast thou forsaken me?' and now 'Get thee behind me, Satan,' I'd say 'Do unto others' rocks with the best of them."

I look at him as we pass the donut shop.

Circle around in front of him and check the eyes
for laugh lines. Unlined, he is serious.

"Oak, what does 'Get thee behind me,
Satan,' mean, actually? I mean, pretty much I got
it, but—"

"Come on, Pauly, will ya? It means the same
thing all the rest of it means. Just, y'know, try to
be good if you can. That's all."

"Ah, you," he says, waving me off and walking ahead a few paces. He takes things very seriously, very briefly.

"Y'know, Oakley, you should try harder than
you do. Big brain like you got and all. You could
possibly make something of yourself, if you only
made a little effort."

"Thanks," I say.

"And you could help me out, at the very
least. Combined, we could be killer. You'd be the
brains and I'd be . . . everything else. We'd make
inventions, build cities we'd call Paulytowns,
cure diseases, start our own church, basically
help out all of humanity, and get ourselves stink-
ing rich."

"That's the spirit," I say. "But, maybe tomorrow . . ."

"'Get thee behind me, Satan,'" Pauly says.

There are three basic progressions to the
Whitechurch postchurch experience. A lot of
folks get the hell out. Families piling into cars to
go on one drive or another, seeing leaves in the
hills or grandparents in other towns or real life in
the city. Then a lot more folks ease on down to

King's Diner for what they call brunch which looks suspiciously like their regular menu only they let you pick from either the lunch or the breakfast fare but not both, or over to the Chinese for dim sum brunch which is probably more legitimately a brunch except nobody in this town would be able to tell you whether it was or not.

But by far the most popular postservice worship option is at Rosa's Cantina. On Sundays, in the modest town of Whitechurch, a good many citizens get the feeling that they have been fortified with the goodness of the Lord, and can drop their pants, so to speak, in the comfort of Rosa's.

"'Get thee behind me, Satan,'" Pauly says as we pass Rosa's.

We always laugh about Rosa's, me and Pauly. Rosa's has a stink. Hideous country music comes out of Rosa's. The Christmas lights stay up all year in the windows. The TODAY'S SPECIAL sign has featured the famous ROSA'S RUMP ROAST for so long, there is now a little number in the corner ticking off the days like a hostage crisis. Today is 612. There is a sad and sorry sorry feeling to the place that reaches out and grabs at you like octopus tentacles as you pass it by.

But Rosa's Cantina is a real bar, with real liquor-license concerns that have caused it to be closed down more than once, so we do not go into Rosa's. We mock it instead.

"Wanna hear a poem?" Pauly asks as we pass Rosa's big mirrored front window, with the roses etched all around the edges and mad loud noises blasting out from behind.

"No," I say.

"Right," he says. "Here goes."

## ROSA'S #1

What's

Inside the cantina

Behind the flowers

Inside the cantina

While you're looking in the mirror

They see out at you

But you don't see in at them

I'm not peeking anyway

Just fixing my hair

Probably there ain't even

nobody named Rosa in there

And I find that, while he's reciting his dumb little poem, we are, actually, staring into that mirror window, inching closer, trying to see through, while idiot Pauly and fool Oakley stare back out at us and god-knows-who-else stares from behind them. There is suddenly an awful lot of laughter going on inside that bar.

"Pathetic," I say, pushing off and heading down Main Street.

"Well, it's not my best work maybe, but that's a little harsh, I think."

"Not the poem. The dopes in the bar."

"Whew," Pauly says, as if my liking the poem was important. "So you *like* the poem," he says.

"No," I say.

He catches up to me, then passes me, walking faster now. "Church makes you bitchy," he says.

"No. *White*church makes me bitchy," I say.

His turn to be snide.

"So leave, then."

This is a joke. It's a bad joke but, anyway, a joke. There is nothing to keep me here. But whenever I consider the alternatives . . . I stop bad-mouthing Whitechurch is what I do. I can't decide whether I'm lazy or chicken, though I suppose the distinction hardly matters in the end.

"Wait," Pauly says, stopping me right there on the sidewalk. He covers his eyes with one hand, and his heart with the other. Pauly's had a vision, which does not thrill me.

## ROSA'S #1.5

When they do finally let me
I'm gonna bring a date in
And I'll say to them all
Get thee behind me Satan

Maybe he's right. Church makes me bitchy. "Even Satan deserves better than that. You weren't going to be satisfied until you worked that into a poem, were ya?"

He shrugs. "I do kind of feel fulfilled now, yes."

"I hate it when you're all cheery right on top of church," I say. But I don't hate it at all.

He finds this funny. On certain days he finds all things funny. "What, are you implying I'm sometimes not cheery?"

We aren't half a block past Rosa's when we hear the crash, the tremendous thunk of the big oak door flying open, banging off the frame of the building, followed by the tumble out of a whole crowd of drinkers tagging after a fight. A loud, messy fight.

"Cool," Pauly says, pulling me by the shirt. But I'm not really in the mood. I tug out of his grip and follow sluggishly behind. Pauly's at a trot, but I take my time, running through the sequence of events about to unfold in a classic savage Whitechurch bar brawl. First, one fat guy is going to shove the other guy, who is probably built a little more slightly, but with a similar hard round beach ball of a stomach. He's going to bark a lot of angry words, having to do with his Slovak heritage, or the condition of our public schools, or hockey. Then he'll shove him again, then again, then at the point where in a real place he would punch the guy, he will inexplicably stop. Then the other guy will rebut whatever the first guy said or actually say much the same things, but in a voice that sounds like he's violently disagreeing. They will get really close to each other and the crowd will politely murmur rather than shout because it is Sunday after all and we do have our Sunday blacks on. The waitress will follow the action out into the street and continue to serve buffalo wings and fried mozzarella sticks and take drink orders. Wives will beg fat men to either stop fighting or intervene to stop the fighting. Eventually, having run out of alternatives, the two guys will be forced to engage each other, grabbing, grappling, poking, then rolling into a heap on the ground. Then Wendell, the full-time police officer, will come to them if he is not at his camp up at Moosehead Lake. If he is at Moosehead, one of the part-timers will step up, tell the guys to cut it out, and they will. Usually somebody has to save face by stomping off home, but often enough everybody will just ooze back into the bar. That winds up being the one piece of intrigue in these things, whether somebody's going to wind up stomping off home, and if I cared, I would be in luck because I come up to the action just about the right time for the exciting cliffhanger conclusion, I figure.

I figure wrong, though. We don't have two of the regulars here.

In fact there is hardly any buzz at all here, the crowd standing more or less dumbfounded watching a real fight. Not a Whitechurch fight. Not a TV Western saloon brawl with chairs and bottles breaking harmlessly over heads and guys being thrown sliding over polished bartops while the player piano tinkles merrily along. Nope.

"I didn't even realize he was in town," I say as I take up my spot alongside Pauly.

The young hard-looking guy looks slightly embarrassed as he stands there in boxing stance, ready to do whatever. Hair grows thick from the backs of his hands, all the way up over his big ropy forearms. You can barely make out the faded blue of his tattoo in the forest of hair. I think it's a girl swinging on a crescent moon.

"We have to get in there. We have to do something," Pauly says to me. "How do you want to do it? Whatever you want, Oak."

My father stands there wobbly. Bloated, very white, bald-headed Dad, his mouth all bleeding, so you can see a small red vivid frame around each tooth as he speaks. He has good teeth still. Nice and white. Always a source of pride with my dad, taking care of his teeth. Flossing, using smokers' toothpaste even though he doesn't smoke. Beautiful teeth.

"Take it back," Dad says to the man. "Or I'll break your fuckin' skull."

"We don't do anything," I say to Pauly.

"For Chrissake," the guy says to Dad, "just fuckin' drop it."

"I'll fuckin' drop you," Dad says. Wisdom and wit being the family hallmarks.

*Crrrack*, you can hear it echo through the valley as the man hits my father dead in the mouth. Couldn't blame him really. He waited as long as he could, then my slow old man tried to sucker him. I'd have done the same thing. Not that I have anything against my dad. Just the way it goes.

He really should let me know, when he's going to be in town. Should call or drop me a postcard at least.

"What's wrong with you?" Pauly says to me, squinching his face all up like there's a bad stink and he can't figure the source of it. I can feel and see looks all around me that are saying roughly the same thing. Some people start slipping back inside.

"What?" I say.

"What, *this*," he says, making a sweeping gesture over me, head to foot. "You're like, nothing."

"Nothing I can do," I say.

He shakes his head at me, turns back toward the fight. I take inventory over the territory Pauly has just highlighted, and I realize I am all over something between pins-and-needles and nothing at all.

"Go home, Artie," Pauly yells at Dad.

Dad looks. "You. You're the goddamn problem, ya little shit. Standin' together in the window, like a coupla . . . he's half right about you."

"Go home, Artie," Pauly says, unfazed.

"More than half," the other guy says.

Dad takes a big awkward sweeping swing at the guy, throws himself way off balance, and nearly falls.

Nearly. Can't even manage to fall properly, which would have been something, anyway. Instead he does this ass-up little pirouette thing, landing on his feet but with his palms pressed flat to the pavement. My father is now showing the crack of his behind to Whitechurch.

I flash on a cold small thought. One of those joke postcards. Whitechurch says hello. My father's smiling white ass.

He refuses to wear a belt. We have discussed it, but still he refuses.

The guy walks over toward Dad to finish him up, and Dad's son feels not a twitch of an impulse to step over there. Lazy or coward? Maybe just smart. Why argue? Let nature take its course. My guiding principle.

Pauly does not subscribe to my guiding principle. Or anyone else's.

"Can't let you do that," Pauly says, sliding his thin self between the men. Every bit as tall as the hard man, Pauly looks still like a child next to him.

"I ain't never hit a girl before," the guy says. "Get outta the way or be hurt."

Pauly stands there and smiles. Not a confident smile, or cocky or anything. Just kind of cosmically amused. A fatal smile perhaps.

"Pauly," I call, suddenly moved, alarmed. "Come on."

"You heard the queen, go sit down."

Pauly points at the man, like he's practicing for our revival show. "'Get thee behind me, Satan.'"

From behind him, my father hops to his feet and smacks Pauly aside. He then hits the guy a solid bang on the jaw.

But the punch does nothing. As the guy rears back, Paul straightens up and absorbs the shot, right on the button, and goes down. The guy reloads and drops Dad immediately thereafter.

There is pretty much nobody left on the street when Wendell, who is not at Moosehead, gives the guy a choice between getting the hell outta Dodge and getting the hell into the cage, which would be nothing but a big pain in the ass for Wendell. The guy chooses to vacate.

"Everybody all right here?" Wendell asks. Dad and Pauly are sitting on the sidewalk. Paul's nose is bleeding and Dad is wiggling two front teeth. They nod. Wendell goes into Rosa's Cantina.

I walk over to them. "You all right?" I ask. Dad just looks down at the ground.

"Did you see me?" Pauly asks, as if he's just pulled off a triple somersault with a twist rather than putting his face in front of a fist. He is smiling nuttily.

Gorgeously.

Nothing you can do with the boy some days. He beams up at me, the blood from his nose pooling around his chin. I offer him a hand up. "You got every guy in town fighting for your honor, bitch," he says. "And yet you pick me."

"Shut up," I say. Unfortunately he knows I don't mean it.

"Nobody calls my boyfriend 'queen' and gets away with it."

"Shut up."

"I'm feeling tough. Let's go get a steak. Oakley, you wanna go get a steak? I got a few bucks—let's go eat."

I look down at my dad, who is still sitting, fingering his teeth. They look brilliant. But they look like they're stuck in the mouth of a mushy jack-o'-lantern about a month past Halloween. He stares down at the sidewalk.

"You wanna come?" I say to him.

He pauses. "Does *he* have to come?"

I nod.

"Maybe next time then," he says.

He's not a bad guy, I swear.

We leave him there.

If any of this at all lowers Pauly's elevated mood, he doesn't show it.

"We'll get something to eat," he chirps, still within hearing distance of Dad, "and then after-wards we'll go someplace and I'll hump ya."

"Jesus, Pauly."

"Fine then, you can hump me this time. But don't get too used to it."

I have lost the impulse to tell him to shut up,

and as we step into the diner we are on the same page.

"'Get thee behind me, Satan,'" we both say, pulling stares from every booth.

# WILL

"YOU GAVE YOURSELF A HAIRCUT."

"I did." He isn't embarrassed in the least. Even though the haircut not only *looks* like he did it himself, it also looks like he did it without aid of a mirror, and that instead of scissors he used a serrated knife.

"Sit in the chair," I bark. We are in my house. My house is an apartment. My apartment, which I share with my dad sometimes but not right now, is above a former coffee shop. It's not a great apartment, but it smells pretty good.

"I hate the smell up here," Pauly says.

"Get in the chair."

Now he's laughing. He likes it when I get all upset and motherly.

"Assuming I get in the chair, what is going to happen to me?"

"What's gonna happen is that you are going

to get a halfway decent haircut so I won't be even more embarrassed than usual to be seen with you on the street. And then, if we achieve that, then maybe we will take my dad's VA check and cash it at the bank and just maybe, if you're real convincing, you'll be able to convince me why I should buy two train tickets."

He sits in the chair. I go rooting around in the odds-and-ends drawer, one down from the silverware drawer and one up from the dishrag and Drano drawer, looking for scissors. They are not particularly sharp, my all-purpose round-tipped scissors with the orange plastic grips and glue bits tracing up and down the blades. But I am certain I can make him look better than he does.

I walk over and stand behind Paul and we both now look into the mirror, which is above the sink which for no apparent reason is right there in the front room by the window that looks out over Main Street.

"I love that you love me like this," Pauly says. Partly that's a boring hairdresser joke, partly that's Pauly saying whatever he can think of to get me off balance and partly it's this thing where we are alone and in close proximity and well, it is just a thing with him.

And just maybe he's trying to divert my attention from what I'm seeing.

It is not instantly noticeable, because of its location, but it is quite noticeable now, up close. Long and angry and just now fully clotted, the slash runs maybe three inches along Pauly's hairline, tracing it perfectly from the right temple down the side of his head, stopping just before the ear. Doesn't look like any incidental slip of the shears. Or rather it could have started out as that, and then the shearer neglected to stop carving.

"What you want to go doing that to yourself for, Pauly?" I hear it come out, sadder than I mean it too.

He pops up out of the chair. "You can be a real freak sometimes, you know that, Oakley? Know what, maybe *you're* the dangerous one. Maybe I should be worried about *you* wielding a pair of scissors. Cutting myself . . ." He spins, walks three paces away from me, spins, walks three paces back. "You know, if you could make use of that kind of imagination you might actually *make* something of yourself."

He stares at me, I stare at him. He gets back in the chair.

I find it easier to speak to his mirror reflection. "But you know, if I ever found out you were doing shit to yourself . . ."

I don't quite know how to finish that.

He starts smirking in the mirror. "Yes? You'll do what?"

I suppose it is rather ludicrous. "I'll kill ya," I say, holding the scissors now like I'm going to stab him.

"Oh ya, that'll teach me."

We both laugh, more out of relief than anything.

"Anyway," he says, "even if you did have the strength, which you don't, and the anger, which you don't, you could never kill me. That would take an act of *will*."

He's finished now, given me both barrels. This is a very big thing with Pauly, because it is what separates him from all the other creatures of the forest, particularly me. He's not bigger or stronger or faster than most people. Or smarter or meaner or more creative.

What it is about Pauly is, it's about will.

He will . . . Pauly will . . . Fill in the blank there and you've got a good chance Pauly *will*. He will do what most of us will not, and that, more than anything else, is what defines him. He has got the will, and will probably find the way.

"Fine," I sigh. "So I won't kill you."

"Thanks, buddy. I probably won't kill you either. Cut my hair?"

"Ya." I start clipping.

He starts musing. A haircut will do that for a person. "Town'd be happy if you did kill me though."

"I don't think even that would make this town happy."

"Never mind the town," Pauly says, "you'd be happy."

"Oh ya, I'd be psyched."

"I'm not kidding, Oakley. You might not want to admit it, but I think sometimes you believe things would be a shitload easier on you if I would just be gone."

"Shut up, Pauly."

"I don't blame you."

"Shut *up*," I yell, and as soon as I do I wonder why. "Pauly," I say calmly, "You're talking crap, okay? If that's what you're gonna do, then just keep quiet during the haircut."

He tries to comply. Lasts about twenty seconds.

"Just concerned with the happiness of my friends," he mutters.

I take a big snip of hair from over one ear, check out the balance, and take a big snip off the other side.

"Which is why we're gonna go to Boston. To look after Lilly's happiness."

I'm staring at the back of his head, wondering how he could have made such a mess of it. And I don't mention all the little scissor-bite marks that make his neck look like it was attacked by Alfred Hitchcock's birds.

"Pauly, what's this haircut, like a computer virus—the more you try and fix it the worse it gets?"

"Can't you just cut it without talking about it? Anyway, don't you want to hear about Lilly's happiness? It's about Decision Weekend. She's going down to the college. You know, they show them around, let them party for a couple of days, then the student decides to sign up. So Lilly's already really decided she wants to go, but figures she'll take the weekend trip anyhow, free vacation, plus she'll get one last look around before committing."

"Are these your sideburns?" I ask. "They look like sideburns, but I don't think they're growing out of your face so much as just pulled down—"

"They're sideburns. Leave 'em."

"So we'll all take the train together then. That'll be a ball."

"Hell no," Pauly says, like I'm the biggest fool. "She didn't, like, *invite* us. Duh."

"So why are we going? Duh."

"To help."

"To h—? Pauly? Pauly, no."

"She needs protection. She's a naive big ol' country gal. She can't be left—"

"Yes she can."

"I see," Pauly says, and bounces a hard and serious V-shaped frown off the mirror. "So you don't really love her then."

"Christ, Paul. Spying. You're spying on Lilly. This is not about Lilly's happiness, it's about your freakishness."

There, I've done it. I know I've done it before I've even finished.

"Stop pouting, Paul."

"I'm not pouting."

"Jesus, we're both looking straight into the same mirror. You're pouting. Cut it out. You're not the victim here, you're the troublemaker."

"*Trouble*maker?"

"Yes, you are winding up for a classic Pauly caper, and I think you should just leave it alone. Let her go, Paul."

And there, I've done it big time. *Let her go.*
Kind of a theme, that one. She's going, to college
in the fall, to the world, away from Whitechurch,
whether Pauly likes it or not. Whether I like it or
not. Pauly most definitely does not. I, well, I like
Lilly, and therefore I like what's best for her.
Whether I like it or not.

Pauly will eventually come around to feeling
the same way. He ain't there yet, though. Not by
a ways.

"Let her go?" he asks coldly, giving me a
chance to make up for the mistake.

I decide not to make up for it. "Ya, Paul. Let
her go."

"Request denied," he says, turning his head
from side to side to check out his new look. I'm
not even finished yet, but who can tell? "I'm
going to Boston."

I sigh. "Maybe I'll just say no, then." This
means something because, for all his talk, Pauly
doesn't like to leave Whitechurch much. Doesn't
like to leave it without me at all. Lilly leaving
Pauly, well that's just sensible. Pauly leaving me?
Unimaginable.

"Fine," he says, hostile cool. "It's not like I
would *really* make any trouble anyway, would I?
Nothing much'll happen."

There is a lot going on there in Pauly's words.
You don't even need to know what he's saying—
and a lot of the time it's impossible to know—to
be worried.

"Fine," I say. "So I have to go, to keep an eye

on *you* while you spy on Lilly."

"*Now* you're getting into the spirit," he says, hopping up out of the chair and brushing hairs all over my floor.

One side of his hair looks better than before.

Mr. Linsky, the bank manager, doesn't give me a hard time about cashing Dad's VA check. He never does. Mr. Linsky's feeling—and it's not something I have to guess at, since he comes right out and says it—is that I deserve whatever I can get. Doesn't care much for my father, is what that means. Kind of a funny feeling, to like somebody who hates your own father, unless you yourself hate your own father which plenty of people do, but I don't. Anyway, here's kind of a decent thing: Sometimes I'll cash the check, and when I count the money there's ten or fifteen bucks more on top of what the check was supposed to be. He's a good-enough guy.

Today, though, I get just what's in the check and no more. Well, a little more. In addition to the money, I get a watch-out-be-careful frown from Mr. Linsky, which is related to the company I keep. Giving me money is no problem for Mr. L. Pauly, on the other hand, can smile and be nice as can be and still get looked at as if he's walked into the bank with a mask and a machine gun.

Train station's a little less of a weirdness. Train people don't really seem to care what you're doing as long as you use the train to get there.

"Hello, Mary Martha," I say, and Mary Martha, who loves the sound of her own name because she made it up herself, is thrilled to say hello back. Penelope is her real name. Kind of a judgment call as to whether she has actually improved things much there, but she appears to be a more friendly person since she buried Penelope, so I suppose it's Whitechurch's gain.

"Boston," she sighs as she punches out the tickets. "I love Boston. Such a romantic city. Such a smart city."

"Been lately?" Pauly asks her sweetly.

She immediately looks down, at her fidgeting hands with the carefully painted burgundy fingernails. "No, never," Mary Martha says. "Been to Lowell, though."

So.

"You guys meeting Lilly?"

"Why do you ask?" I ask.

"Why do you ask?" Pauly asks, and asks in such a way as to wipe me out entirely. He is now at the counter, collecting the tickets I paid for. He's leaning close to Mary Martha.

"'Cause she bought tickets on the same run, that's all. Only natural to figure"—and here Mary Martha allows herself a dangerous little laugh—"that since you are her boyfriends, that you all'd be going together."

Pauly is more amused than I am. Outwardly, at least.

"You know, Mary," he says, all sweet and intimate-like.

"Martha," she corrects.

"You know, Martha—"

"Mary Martha."

Pauly sighs loudly, but really he's not bothered at all. In fact he could do this kind of thing endlessly. "Listen, Penelope," he says in a voice that can best be described as juicy, "just, if you see Lilly, and if you want to be my friend . . ." He is so close to her, their noses may actually be touching. "Do me the favor of not telling Lilly we're on this train, okay? It's a surprise." He takes the tickets, lingers in her face for a few seconds more.

"Hey," she snaps. There aren't a lot of people in town who do that, who snap at Pauly. It catches his attention. He returns to the desk. "That's not what you were gonna say to me."

There is a green wrought-iron bench with a splintery wooden seat, there next to the ticket counter. This feels like a good time for me to make use of it. I'm not sure what Pauly is up to, but it makes me uneasy and I'd just as soon bug out. The bench is not the most unpleasant spot in town, either, the old-style train platform outside the nice Victorian station house. Always breezy up here, and always smelling of the pines that densely surround it. Perfect for a little respite from the business of Paul.

"Okay," Pauly says, now that she has enticed him back into the conversation by being like him. "What I was saying, Mary Martha,"—he makes a proud and charming little nod to her at the feat of getting her names right—"is that I've been thinking about you lately. How there's something different about you since you became *Mary Martha* . . ."

Moving to the bench does me no good. I'm still within range, and I'm still pretty well hooked. I mean, he's a pretty disturbing creature, more or less to the entire population of the town. But the thing is, people seem to be altogether ready to be taken by him, when it's the one-to-one thing. Which, I suppose, explains me even more than it does anybody else. I'm his greatest friend, greatest supporter, greatest victim.

"Funny, Mary Martha, but it was just on the way over here that me and Oakley were talking about this very thing"—he sounds warm, as if rekindling an old intimacy—"about how it might be cool to get to know you better, to maybe hang out some."

Of course we never discussed any such thing. But I half believe him myself.

"Shut up," Mary Martha says.

Fair-enough response, I figure. But then there is more under there. We all know it. That's his gift, the underneath he seems to know for no good reason. Like lunatics, the way they can sense stuff. Even though Pauly's not nuts.

"Shut up," she repeats. "You were not talking about me. Liar." Mary Martha leans way far out over her safe little counter and stares straight down at me, Oakley, who for whatever reason has developed a sort of rep for telling the truth.

"Hi, Mary Martha," I say.

Which seems to be enough for her. "Liar," she says to him, in such a coy way that she really could have said any number of finer things.

"Just two days," Pauly says. "Think about it . . . think about it. . . . Trains, y'know? Of course you know. Who knows better than you do what can happen to people on trains? They take you places even before you get there, don't they? You see people coming and going all the time. Shit definitely happens to those folks, don't you think, Mary Martha formerly known as Penelope?"

Mary Martha has a rabbit look about her, as if she will bolt right from her little post right this second.

"Pauly." I reach over and tug on his shirt sleeve. "What are you doing, numbnuts? Lilly, remember? Lilly. *Lilly*, for crying out loud. What do you have to be doing this to Mary Martha for?"

I think I have accomplished this much: I have stalled the process long enough for Mary Martha to regain her balance, if not her sanity.

She waves him off. "Some of us work, you know." Pause. "You're crazy, you know that?"

He leans toward me and whispers. "We're just playing with each other. She understands. I'm not really trying to make her go." Then, with hardly a flicker of a channel change, he turns it on, on Mary Martha. "Girl, I am not crazy. I am a poet."

She wags a finger at him. "Wait a sec, I think I heard about this."

"Stand back," Pauly says dramatically.

## MARY MARTHA #7

Destination

Desperation

From her little

choo choo station

She watches the goer

and comer

Will you be a singer

or sad scared little

hummer?

She takes a step back from the counter and claps her hands three times. "Hah," she says. "Cute. And, ah, number *seven*? You're trying to tell me you perpetrated seven of those things on me?"

He nods solemnly, bows.

"So great, you're a liar *and* a loon."

"Hey," Pauly says, "don't forget, liar plus loon equals poet."

He is backing away. He stops backing away, approaches the counter once more. "Fascination/Inspiration/The poet's muse/the girl at the station.

Why did you change your name, Mary Martha?"
He asks sincerely.

She has no intention of answering, or speaking at all, judging from the look on her face. Narrow-eyed. Blushing. Then, just as quickly, different. Opening. Ready . . .

"No," Pauly says, as if he too has had a very abrupt change of heart. "No, tell me later, when we meet again. And maybe I'll trade you . . . 'Mary Martha #3,' 'Mary Martha #9 . . .'"

"Nine," she repeats dubiously.

Then, as he suggested, she stops, but hangs there, on the edge of something. There is a kind of dewey look to her now, and I think, as I stand and get more of a full-on angle, that Mary Martha is not the least attractive person in Whitechurch. She's not, in fact, unpretty at all.

We back away, smiling, waving. We board the train and start heading to the rear.

"What you doing that for, Pauly?" I ask. "All that with Mary Martha. Teasing her up like that. What's she ever done to you?"

"What are you talking about?" Pauly is distracted as he talks, looking all over the place. "I didn't do anything bad."

"You did. You got a girlfriend. And you're going to see her, and you're gonna see her in Boston, even though you're not even invited and it's gonna make shitloads of trouble for all parties."

"You know, Oakley, did it ever occur to you that I wouldn't be nuts if only you would show a little more faith in me, huh?"

I pause. "You are not nuts," I say.

And the words ring and ring again in my head like an echo of a scream in the valley of Whitechurch. I hear the words, and I think about everything, and I am suddenly, physically tired.

And weary of selling this.

"Well, nice try anyway. But thanks."

The train is about to go. Train noises come out of it. A bell rings, and some goof in a flat-headed train-guy hat starts yelling. Pauly looks suddenly desperate.

I smack him. "Dodo, don't cry. I'm sure she got on the train already."

He then smacks himself. Lilly is never, ever, late for anything, trains, movies, walks in the park, nothing. We, on the other hand, are late all the time.

Paul smacks me, once we are moving and he's loosening up. "And don't call me dodo," he says.

So here's what we do. We crouch low and skulk all cloak-and-dagger trying not to be seen as we head for the rear car. Why?

"Because she's gonna just die from the surprise when we meet her there. The train would be too easy."

"And Lilly dying is what we *want*, is that it?"

He pulls me by the arm, through three cars on the ugly old oily old Amtrak diesel as we head for the last seats in the last car. We pause, like a couple of criminals, each time we exit one car and are about to enter another. To take a quick peek.

It's a funny feeling, this hiding-from-somebody jazz, very foreign, very made-up and play-actish. Because, it occurs to me, Pauly and I slither and pound the streets of Whitechurch day after day, visible to all, but the feeling is nobody notices, cares, or half the time sees us. Now that we're headed out, where we should be anonymous, it's the other.

We stop short before entering the rear car. We are standing on that steel-mesh grate above the apparatus linking the two cars, and we just hover there for a few seconds. Not because we have to—the car is absolutely empty—just because we do. The wind is hard and slashing. The train feels twitchy, as if it is bolting through a line of tacklers who keep trying to knock it off track from either side, like there is a force working against us getting to our destination, but that force is wasting its time. Fifty million trees shoot by at fifty million miles per hour and the clean biting north-country air mixes with the greasy Amtrak air and that's what we breathe. Train-ride breathing.

"I love this shit," Pauly says, taking it in deep. He has stopped completely, and turns around to face me. His eyes are closed. I'm about to echo his statement when he decides to add another. "And I love you, cocksucker."

He's banging me in the chest with his pointer finger as he says it.

I'm really mad now, though I cannot quite figure what is setting me off. I think I'm going to scream at him and throw him off the train, but I can't decide in which order.

"I *paid* for these tickets," I scream into the wind, and all he can do is laugh at me before turning and sliding open the door to the rear car. I let the door slice between us rather than follow. Giving myself a few seconds before going on. Pauly knows I'm doing this, probably already knew I would, and does not wait. He heads straight for the back, and sits in the bench that faces me.

I let the wind beat me this way and that, close my eyes like Pauly did, suck it all up. Feel like I could ride like this for a while. But then without warning, it starts pissing down rain. Like it seems to do every damn day around here unless it snows.

I take the seat facing Pauly, as the seats are all face-to-face, like Amtrak has some kind of investment in people getting to know each other.

He's looking out the window, and I know what he's thinking. "I read it rains every day in Hawaii," I say, pleasantly enough to sound plausibly optimistic, but not so much I sound like a dimwit.

He turns on me. "You see any goddamn palm trees out that window?"

I do not look out the window. I know what is and is not out the window. "Don't say love and cocksucker to me in the same sentence, all right?" I finally say.

"Oh, Christ," he says, looking over my shoulder.

Again, I don't need to look. "Guess we shouldn't be rushing into the private-eye business, huh Pauly?"

He continues staring, tries smiling without looking guilty, does not. I can feel her hovering over my shoulder. And I am not displeased. Not displeased that she's here, that she's found us, and not displeased that Pauly's squirming.

"Have a seat, Mary Martha," he says.

Okay then, this is different.

"Jesus," I say.

"What's up with you?" Mary Martha asks, smiling. "I thought this was a party."

"Who's watching the station?" I ask her, as if that's really my problem.

"Lilly," she says with a giggle.

"*Lilly*?" Pauly and I both gasp. We scramble to the window as if we can catch a last glimpse of her at the station, which we can't. We can imagine Lilly laughing at us, waving, flipping a finger, perhaps.

Pauly throws himself back into his seat and mounts a major pouting campaign.

I sit once again across from him. "Hey, don't be antisocial," I say, finding myself suddenly, uncharitably cheery.

"Ya, it's a party, remember?" Mary Martha says.

"Ya, well who invited you?" Paul wants to know.

"Duh," Mary Martha says.

"You told Lilly," he says.

"Duh," she says.

"Good for you, Mary Martha. Take no prisoners. Take no shit."

"Take a hike," Paul says to me, and it feels more like a party every minute. I could like this. Lilly's out of the picture, so I can stop sweating that and I can admit how much that was eating at me. Mary Martha has called Pauly's bluff and now he's got to deal with it. He's going to have to make up eight more poems pretty quick.

For once, Pauly's made to reap what Pauly has sown. For once, I am free and clear.

Mary Martha means business too. "You were so nice a few minutes ago. Are people right about you, psycho boy?"

Pauly cuts such a look at her now, I'm myself taken aback, which ain't good. He's dark here, head pointed down, eyes turned up, so the effect is like he's lighted from below, eye whites scary white set in dark dark socket holes.

"Who calls me psycho boy? Tell me who, and I'll go to their house and gouge out their hearts. I am not psycho."

Points for ol' Mary Martha. She gets the joke even before I do.

"Knew you were going to say that," she says.

The lights come back on all over his face which, when you are here close up and liking him, you can see, is about the most open and touchable face you could find. He loves it when people are not worried by him. Even better than when they are.

"How come you changed your own name?" Pauly.

"How come you cut your own hair?" Mary Martha.

"Hah." Me.

"I didn't do this," Paul says. "It was him."

Mary Martha looks at me. "I thought you two were friends."

"Tickets, please" is what we hear now. The conductor comes to collect. We all give up our tickets, and the guy whips out his little doohickey that puts a million holes in the tickets. When he's done with me and Pauly, he stares at Mary Martha like a disapproving father. Disapproving of *us* we can assume.

"Hi, Chet," she says pleasantly.

"Hi," he says, and punches her ticket so many times there's more of it on the floor than in her hand.

"So what happened?" Pauly wants to know.

"Buy me a drink first and I'll tell you."

Pauly laughs. He loves to be pushed around like this. Then he looks to me. The money, remember.

"Fine," I say, because I am truly getting in a party mood. I feel light, like there's nothing on me. Pauly's the one at work now. Think I might like the switch today, me playing Pauly trouble-maker, while he tries to clean up his own mess. "Lemme just run to the dining car and see what I can do." But before I can go I have one thing to do.

"Hey, Paul," I say, pointing at him. "Recite Mary Martha that poem you just told me. You know, 'MM #23.'"

I don't wait for the reaction. Work like that is its own satisfaction.

And off I go, even though what I can do is probably nothing more than grab a lemonade since I'm a few years short of legality yet. So what, thinks I, whatever it is will be fun enough. I feel an unusual lightness, a nothingness. And I'm liking it.

Out the first car door I go, and there I pause because the rain has gone, quick as it came. Watching the ties hammer past through the grate beneath my feet. Feeling the wind, smelling the diesel pine. Nice. A few faces scattered through- out the next car, everybody sleepy, nobody friendly exactly, but nobody a bother either. Fair enough. Nothingness undisturbed. Outside the second car, same pause, same nice, through the door, into the dining car.

Nothingness disturbed.

Her. The flower girl of Whitechurch, the one I've never been able to talk to, with the eyes and the hair and the whiteness beyond belief and the big-eye stare. She recognizes me, I think, or she thinks I'm somebody else and I absolutely do not care which.

She has snapdragons, real branches of honey-suckle and other wildflowers not indigenous to Whitechurch, tangled into the already nuts tangle of her peach-colored hair. She is like one colorized player walking through the black-and-white film I always seem to be watching, and living. And her every brief appearance makes me start to think, again, that I sure would like to step out of this film and into that one. I hardly feel my feet beneath me, a sensation made all the worse by the persistent side to side to side to side shimmy of the train every inch of the way. I have to look down at my sorry feet to even know that I have stopped dead.

I think I'm smiling at her. I know she is smiling at me, and that is all the encouragement I should need. This is where I should step through, finally, into that world, even for just a small while, and see if it's maybe a world I could love.

But there is something else. There is a something that carves its way into this vision, that prevents this, and I know damn well what it is. And there is no way I can pull this off here and now without simultaneously ruining it.

I must look like I'm going to cry as I wave to her and back away. I must look it because I feel it. I flee. Back, through the sliding doors, through the previous car and the previous doors and back to the party, which feels suddenly a lot less like one.

Whatever did happen to that lightness I felt? How is it that things can turn so quickly, and on such small occurrences as a girl simply appearing on the same train to Boston?

I am dizzy enough from it all that I am back with Paul and Mary Martha without feeling as if

I've even moved. She is laughing hysterically.

"You are so bad," she says, slapping me on the arm, "making him do that filthy poem for me." She looks to Pauly.

He, of course, is beaming with pride. Chalk up another one.

"Where are the drinks?" he says.

I stare at him. That's all I feel like doing. Not true. I am wishing I were a magnifying glass, and the sun was searing behind me, pinpointing Paul through my eyes.

"To hell with the drinks," Mary Martha says. "I got smoke. Why don't we just smoke instead?"

I never smoke. I do not like the way it makes me feel. The lightness without the well-being. The scary feeling of no control, even worse than the everyday feeling of no control.

"Sure," I say.

This throws Pauly nicely. He takes a good sharp look into me. The three of us are out the back now, on the small platform where the car we were riding would be attached to the car that was following, if there were more than ten or twelve people ever desiring to travel to or from Whitechurch by train. Pauly is staring at me, tilted, the way a dog does when you make an unfamiliar sound. The wind feels wild and screamy, the way it seems to rush from all sides, swarming us and whipping our hair onto our faces as we face out the back toward where we were. Somehow Mary Martha manages to light up, and she is pulling hard on the smoke.

"Mary Martha here says Lilly didn't get on the train because of me," Pauly says as if he's talking about the banner headline on the morning's *Whitechurch Spire*. He takes the joint and sucks on it, then continues talking. "Says Lilly already made up her mind about school anyway. She's gone, Oak. What do you think about that?"

He passes me the joint as if he's passing me the info. I take it, I stare at it. The flower girl is perhaps now in the dining car gifting somebody else with her smile. I take a minor hit of the joint.

"So what, Pauly?" I say. "We knew this, I think. We knew Lilly was going. She wants a life, and she doesn't need your permission. It would probably be a good time to stop playing stupid about it." Normally this moment would be *handle with care*. Trouble is, at this moment, I don't. Care.

I stare at him, provoking. I hope he screams at me.

"My favorite color is VCR blue," Paul says evenly.

Mary Martha snorts a laugh, grabs a smoke. "Recite another Mary Martha poem," she says.

"The color of the screen when the tape is finished but you leave the TV on. I watch that for hours sometimes."

I take the joint from Mary Martha before she offers it. I take another hit. What a chump I was not to go to her. I should go back to the bar and invite her back here, is what I should do.

I'm thinking, I did it again.

I'm thinking, He wasn't even there, for Chrissake.

I'm thinking, I can't remember when it wasn't like this.

I'm thinking, Thinking is a start anyway.

I'm thinking, I may well do it. I'm thinking hard on it when Pauly snatches the smoke from the pinch of my fingers, and Mary Martha works at sparking up a second one.

"Mary Martha keeps making me offers I shouldn't be able to refuse," Pauly says, nervous-grinning. "And listen to this, she says that Lilly says it's fine with her if I go for it."

Weird, I am glad to hear that Lilly said that. Go, Lilly.

Run, Lilly.

"Why did you change your name, Mary Martha?" I ask.

"Why would Lilly say that?" Pauly asks. Suddenly adrift.

Mary Martha looks at me. "How come you don't have a girlfriend, Oakley? Good-looking guy like you, and nice, too, not like this psycho-path Pauly."

"That's not my name anymore," Pauly says. "I want to be called Penelope."

"Shut up, Pauly," she says, and hits him very sharply, very affectionately, on the shoulder. I feel bad for Mary Martha.

"Okay, you can still call me Pauly, but it's the other one, the one spelled P-o-l-l-y."

"How come, Oakley?" she persists.

*How come.* How come? Why does that phrase mean "why"? Like, how did it come to this? Is that it? How, fucking, come?

"Because he's got *me*," Pauly says.

"Didn't Mary Martha ask you for a poem a while back? Ya fake," I say.

I figure to catch him off guard, make him slip. As so many times before, I figure him wrong. He leans with his back against the rail, facing me head-on.


## Mary Martha—Epilogue

Dear Miss Penelope

This is all hell for me

The color

is VCR

It's not a bad haircut

It's a scar

Now the death flower's

fading

Love does not fucking last

But say now

This train's trucking

awfully fast


Mary Martha is game, but also inexperienced and stoned. She does her best.

"Was I in there someplace?" she asks, then chuckles.

All I know at the moment is that I am not, in there. I don't care what is, either. Pauly is right about me. If something requires an act of will, I won't.

That has to stop.

I will ask the flower girl to join us.

The conductor's face appears in the window, and suddenly I am in a full panic. We will be arrested now. I know we will be, and I hate that feeling so much. We were arrested before, me and Pauly. I used my phone call to bring my dad down, and luckily he was home to do it and to not give a particular shit about it either which is not too bad a quality in a father I think. Pauly used his one call to call, as he said, the only person he had.

He called me. Right there at the police station while I sat in the cage. He lifted the number when they were interviewing him at the desk.

The cops didn't think it was all that funny once they worked it out. I thought it was pretty all right once I did.

I point at the face, and Mary Martha turns to check. She pounds the glass and he goes away.

"Don't mind these people here. I'm an employee, remember. And if you had any idea what these boys put inside themselves . . . you'd *walk* to Boston."

"I don't want to go to Boston," Pauly says.

I know in an instant he is cemetery serious.

"Are the drivers really screwed up all the time? Do you think we really might crash?" Pauly has swung around to the side of the train, looking forward into the mad wind. He is leaning way far out, the way they told you not to as a kid or a pole would tear your head off. I'm suddenly aware of the *sound* of the train as I watch Pauly. Like the noise is the soundtrack to his actions, and that noise is like the assault of drummers on the street, a hundred drummers on the street, banging and banging away on big metal cans, going faster, then faster, then harder, until they've gotten inside you, beating from inside you.

Mary Martha still thinks this is a conversation. "Nah, I was just—"

"I don't sleep with anybody but Lilly," Pauly says, and he is saying it to me. Then to Mary Martha. Actually, he's screaming it, fighting the wind. "I want to see Lilly. I don't want to see Boston. I don't sleep with anybody besides Lilly."

He doesn't. Doesn't sleep with anybody besides Lilly. Nor with Lilly herself.

Now it sounds like helicopters. Like beating blades of helicopters are coming up from beneath our feet. I look down. Then up at Pauly. Then down again, like I cannot tell which of these things is really happening.

"Don't hang so far over there, Pauly," I say.

"Pole'll take your head off," Mary Martha says.

His only acknowledgment is to bare his teeth.

His mouth blows wide open and distorted and he hyperventilates, hissing in and out between his teeth.

We come tearing through an old mail depot, and the poles now do come whipping past, one-two-three-four, swings of giant bats just missing Pauly's head. I recoil with every one. Mary Martha gasps. Pauly fails to notice us. He's treating the poles the way a bullfighter treats bulls, leaning into them, daring them, yapping at them.

Until I yank him back in.

"Cut the shit," I say.

For all the world, he appears to be answering a statement I didn't make. "You think so? Oakley, you don't really believe that, that she's gone."

Fortunately he's not looking for a response from me, because I am empty. He turns toward the back railing. The smoke is all gone, which is probably good. The wind and mainly fresh air are still with us, which is good. Poles don't tear heads off from the back of the train.

"Relax, Pauly," I say. "Boston's not that far away from Whitechurch."

"But it *is*," he snaps. "It's *all* the way away. Do you understand me? It is all the way away, and if I go, then I don't get back. You understand?"

I don't. But I haven't given it a great effort either. He will uncoil on his own. "No, Paul," I say. "I don't understand."

Mary Martha doesn't either. "You aren't half the fun you'd figure to be, Pauly."

He is hanging over the back rail, and I fear he is going to get sick. I step right up next to him, same hunched posture, shoulder tight up against his. The tracks are flying past beneath us. And the river is flying past beneath that. Our unbeautiful river is not quite brown. Tawny, you'd call it, tawny and flat as it flies by below us as if it actually had a life of its own, rather than just the illusion of motion created by the train's real motion. Me and Pauly are both looking at it the same long way.

"Ever see *Butch Cassidy and the Sundance Kid*?" he says, looking up and crookedly smiling at me. The words are not the problem. The crooked smile and the nearly imperceptible bouncing up and down on the balls of his feet is not the problem. It's the sudden hungry thrill in the squint of his eyes. That's the problem.

"No, Paul."

"It's about these two buddies in the old—"

"No. I mean, no, we are not jumping."

"Ah, hello?" Mary Martha says. "Is this a private party?"

Pauly looks over his shoulder at her. He speaks in a loud confessional whisper. "Are you a virgin, Mary Martha? Was Penelope a virgin? Or like, with a new name did you get to start over again?"

"Right. I'm getting in out of the rain," Mary Martha says. It is not raining. She goes inside and shuts the sliding door.

"Maybe we should rob trains and stuff.

Better than staying behind in Whitechurch, huh?"

He is hanging far over now, staring down at the railroad ties slamming by beneath our feet. The sound of the drummers backed by high-speed highway traffic, and crashing surf. Pauly's feet are barely touching the platform.

Through all the din, I can still hear myself breathing. Through my nose. Hard, clipped, small explosions of air. I sound more like a train than the train does.

"Why all the *we*, Paul?" I say, finally say. "*We* should jump off, *we* should rob trains. I don't want any of that, okay? You wanna rob a train, *you* rob a fuckin' train."

Now the rain does come. And it comes in torrents.

"And if *I* want to jump?" he asks, and he looks so so pleased with this bend in the conversation, it's as if I have made all the bad things go away.

I'm out over the edge myself now. The rain is coming so heavy it is shoving us downward. The chunky brown railroad ties are rising to meet our faces halfway. I feel the blood coming to my head, pooling behind my eyes, and the sound is now a cattle stampede across a steel surface.

"Go on," Pauly says. His own eyes look swollen, as if the same blood dam is about to burst in him. "Go on and tell me. I'll get you started even. 'Pauly, if you want to jump . . .'"

I turn to him, and our faces are so close the

rain is running off the tip of my nose onto his cheek.

"Can't even make this fuckin' decision without me, can ya, Paul?"

He looks like a corpse. The blood has run out, gone somewhere inside. Cold and fishy in the eye, whiter than bone.

I straighten up. He continues to hang there like a gaffed tuna.

"Where are you going?" he croaks.

"Goin' to get a life, Paul."

I have my hand on the steel handle to the door to the train.

"I love you," he says before I open the door.

"Cocksucker," he says after I open it.

I stand there looking at Mary Martha and the conductor, sitting in the rear seats playing cards. They stare up at me.

"Ah, that didn't mean either of the things you probably think it would."

She shakes her head at me. "People are one-hundred-percent right about you two."

I nod. "Regardless. Will you do me a favor and pull him out of the rain in about five minutes? I have an appointment."

"Okay," she says, and returns to her game. The conductor sneers at me.

I have my hand now on that heavy sliding silver door, looking through that small window right into the sweet open real-life face of that girl, and she is happy to see me too, waving me in and in I am coming, look out now, because I am going to finally step through, join up. . . .

I never open that door.

The engine bucks, like something has bounced off us, then decelerates.

I run hard all the way to the rear of the train once more.

Mary Martha is sitting there, edged up a little closer to the conductor, still playing cards.

"See you back in 'Church, cocksucker," Mary Martha says as I shoot through the rear exit.

The train has jerked to a stop in this the first station on the Boston trip.

I hop down off the back of it and follow after him.

# WATCH

I sit at the window watching the wind blow.
Rather, watching the evidence
of the wind blowing at forty miles per hour.
The mushroom cap of an exhaust unit
on the roof of the bakery
across the street,
spinning like a whirligig,
the trees that grow in a line behind
the main shops of the town,
dipping down below the roof lines,
springing back up,
ducking again,
fighting for position
against the wicked wind we get around here.

Watching from my room, facing the street,
set on the second floor
over the empty shop where up until one month
    ago
they sold fifty different blends of coffee
but now they're gone
because Whitechurch
only ever wanted
one.
And I watch,
across the street and three doors left,
as the big plate glass window of the
    Laundromat
bows, twists, distorts,
tries to pop itself
out of its frame
onto the street.
But I'm not watching that,
even if it is entertaining.
I'm watching
the Red-Headed Stranger,
who is doing his laundry
because it is Wednesday evening,
and as Whitechurch knows
he does his laundry
on Wednesdays.

Tell the truth though, I'm not even watching
    that.
Of course I'm watching it, that is,
the same way I'm watching
the whirligig
and the trees
and the window.
Satellite visions they are,
pulling my eye closer
to the source.
The Red-Headed Stranger struggling
to light a cigarette
with his rain-slicker hood
pulled tight around his face
and his hands cupped against the wind
is *close* to the center,
but not *it*.
*It* is Lilly.
Lilly watching the Stranger.
I am watching Lilly
watching the Stranger.
And then, there is Pauly.
Pauly watching Lilly
watching the Stranger
light a cigarette
in the light of the 'mat.

I'm watching that.

I am the only one watching that.

Because none of the other players

even knows yet

that Pauly is there,

skulking

in the doorway of Chuck's International Auto

    Parts,

watching Lilly

watching the RHS.

Pauly named him that.

After the guy had been in town

a few days

and been the subject

of a few thousand

conversations.

Came out of nowhere

our own red menace,

remains nowhere

even as we

watch.

The only redhead in town,

Lilly observes.

And isn't that queer,

we don't have one

of our own

and we never

noticed

before.

We do now.

We notice.

Which is why Lilly is there,

inside the Laundromat

looking out at RHS,

and Pauly is outside

looking at her,

with the rain

coming down sideways

in the wind,

a little hail mixed in,

bouncing right off Pauly's unmoving face

in the doorway of Chuck's International Auto

    Parts

across the street

one flight down

and three doors over

from my window.

# WHITE RABBIT

I GRAB UP MY ORANGE MACKINTOSH from the hook on the back of the closet door, and go down to the shiny street.

It's just getting dark, and the blue-white fluorescence pours out of the place and highlights Adam Everly, the 'mat's manager, son of Asa Everly, the 'mat's owner. He stands on his stepladder trying to clutch the top rung and at the same time to apply a giant X of tape to the window to keep it from shattering. He's already Xed the inside, but that isn't enough for Adam, who is a good son, a conscientious Laundromat manager, and who is thirty-five years old and otherwise unemployable.

"Hey Adam," I say to our man Adam, who is somehow still more of a kid to the locals.

"Hey," Adam says, but not in a friendly way or even a dead-middle-zone way like I said it, but in an aggressive way.

"It's not my fault you're all wrapped up in tape, Adam."

Adam has been struggling to escape the roll of nylon-reinforced plastic tape, going from the methodical peeling and stretching method to the flailing, growling, thrashing method that only makes tangled tape worse.

"No," Adam says, going limp like a person surrendering to quicksand. "It's not your fault."

The hail, now the size of pencil erasers, is bouncing off my rubberized coat like it is all a planned assault on me alone. It is just the coat for these storms. I stand with my hands in the pockets and nothing on my face as far as I can feel. Just as if I'm still watching the weather from my warm chair—which would be the smart thing—rather than standing in it. I look toward Chuck's International Auto Parts, then past Adam into his dad's business which will be Adam's business once the drink finishes its work on Asa's organs, then back to Chuck's again. Chuck's is a more stable Whitechurch business, as Chuck drinks less than Asa does except when they're together.

"The window's not going anyplace, Adam."

Adam looks up at it, the window, for an answer. "No?"

"No. You did great. I was watching you. The building will fall down, but the window will still be hanging. Sell me a Lotto."

That is the other thing that happens in the Laundromat. Lotto tickets. Asa is diversifying the business. Providing for the kid, who nobody figures stands much of a chance anyway.

"I got the winner tonight," Adam says. "I'll sell it to you. But when you win you gotta buy me dinner at King's. I can feel it. This night's a winner."

He says that every time he sells a ticket.

I buy one anyway. Stand there in my dopey, dripping mac, hand a dollar to Adam, and send him behind his small Formica counter to punch up the numbers machine and make it *buzz-tik-tik-tik-tik-buzzzz*. "You're right," I say as Adam Everly hands over the ticket, "that definitely sounded like a winner."

"So, you gonna take me to King's for dinner when you win?" Lilly says, banging her shoulder into mine. The two of us then lean, side by side, on our elbows and watch Adam do the other thing he does behind the counter. Fold other people's underwear.

Me and Lilly are the same height, five foot ten, and of similar square and gristly build. We could be brother and sister, and people have often said stuff to that effect. Pauly is taller than us by two inches.

"King's is gonna be crowded that night," I say. King's is the best restaurant in town, with a sign in the window to prove it that says BEST RESTAURANT IN TOWN that nobody takes issue with. Except for the food. It's a very nice *place*, just that the food is kind of putrid-tasting. I'm happy enough to have company at my celebratory dinner there, so that when I have to push my plate away after three bites of canned-salmon pie, somebody will be there to help me out. Because the waitresses quiz you when you leave food at King's.

"Hey, Adam," Lilly calls.

Suspiciously, Adam turns his eyes up from the folding. He isn't all that used to being chatted up by most people. Certainly not by the town's Major Young Woman. He makes a nice pleat, Asa says of his boy, but he could bore the fuzz off a peach. "Hey, Lilly," he says back.

"You want me to help you with that? Me and Oakley, we can help you with that, can't we, Oak?"

"No, we can't."

"No, you can't," Adam Everly says, getting busy busy in the whites. The colors sit in a knot behind him. He is diligent about separating. "Nobody's supposed to be touching anybody else's things. 'Specially their underthings," he says super-seriously. "That's one of the sacreds of the business."

"Sacreds, huh?" Lilly says. "You know, you never figure there are sacreds in some businesses. Guess they can pop up anywhere, huh?"

He listens without looking at her. "Yes," Adam Everly says, "I think they can."

Lilly is not convinced. "So let us help anyway. How sacred is sacred?"

Adam Everly is mortified. "Sacred," Adam says. "Sacred is very sacred. This might not be much to you, it might not look like anyth-th-th-thing to you." He starts stuttering. Adam Everly went to a special school for years to fix his stutter, and Lilly is bringing it back by wanting to handle Whitechurch's underthings. "B-b-b-but something has to mean something to a person. It's imp-p-p-portant to *some*body . . . Lilly," he says, then returns to folding.

She stops grinning, looks to me. I point at her like she's a bad girl, which nobody believes. Not even wounded Adam Everly believes it. Bad girl, Lil.

"I like the way you say my name," she says to him. He does not look at her. "L-l-l-lilly. It doesn't even sound wrong when you stutter it. Sounds pretty. Sounds singsongy."

He looks up at her with narrowed eyes and a seedling of a smile. "Your boyfriend. He's always wanting to hold everybody's things too. You're a pair. The two of you," Adam says.

"Hey, lemme fold," Pauly says as he bursts through the door, propelled, as if the storm threw him up. "If these guys get to fold, you gotta let me."

"No," Adam Everly says.

"Adam," Lilly says softly. "Sorry about the underwear thing. You're right, it is important. You're a gent."

"What's the red menace doing here?" Pauly asks, prompting everyone to look. "Is he ever gonna leave?"

"L-l-l-lillly," Adam Everly croons.

Lilly looks away from the Stranger. Opens a sweet grateful sad smile on Adam. "Thank you," she says to him.

Pauly fixes a stare on Adam now. A simple stare. Profoundly simple. There is no one Pauly can't be jealous of.

"L-l-l-lilly," Adam says.

"Don't wear it out, Adam," I say, to be helpful. I like him anyway, but I seem to like him less when I'm with Lilly.

"Sell me a Lotto," Pauly says.

Adam Everly acts as if he hasn't heard this. He curls the last pair of sweat socks up together, even though they look yellow and crusty, as if they were in the In pile rather than the Out.

"Hah, that's Ben Ginty's laundry. No mistaking those socks," Pauly says. Triumphant. "Sell me a Lotto."

Adam Everly. Chivalrous. He scoops up the load of white that may belong to bachelor bricklayer Ben Ginty. Shields the stack with his body and walks it to the rear of the folding area. There he picks up a lump of unfolded colors and brings it to the folding table.

"Sell me a Lotto," Pauly says.

Adam gets angry. Quietly. He stops folding, places his hands flat on the table and stares across at Pauly. Pauly does not make Adam stutter. "One dollar," Adam says.

"Ah," Pauly moans. "I'll pay you two. Out of the winnings."

"Oh ya, *there's* a wise investment," I snort.

"Dad says cash only," Adam Everly says robotically.

"You two small-timers need some serious help," Pauly says. "No guts, no glory boys. Come on Lilly, I wanna go. Let's go for a walk. The air's a little *sluggish* in here."

She looks out the window. "In this? Pauly, you want to go for a walk in *this*?"

"Yes I do."

She looks again. Smiles. "Kinda cool. Unlike you, though."

He looks level at her, which one learns quickly on meeting him is something Pauly seldom does. "I know, unlike me." He's watching the Stranger. "I'm thinking I might dye my hair too, how 'bout that?"

Lilly zips her jacket up to her chin. She pulls her white baseball cap down almost to her ears and shoves Pauly toward the door.

Nobody says see ya later to me. We are beyond all that.

"See ya later . . . L-l-l-lilly," Adam says, as the door fights to close itself against the storm. Adam Everly is not beyond all that.

Nothing in the Laundromat that was interesting is interesting anymore to me. The fizziness is gone. I wrap myself up tight, slap the counter loudly. Adam doesn't look up, the Red-Headed Stranger does. He and I look at each other. Like two dumb cows across a field. We nod at each other, a greeting, a farewell, an acknowledgment, an agreement, one or more of those things a nod is supposed to mean but I honestly wonder sometimes who the hell knows. But anyway, one nod more than we'd ever exchanged while I had company.

I go back out, and across, and up, and into, down into my chair, at the window and above the coffee-scented spaces in the floorboards, to watch the storm and not participate in it.

"Nah, you didn't miss much," I say to my dad, asleep on the sofa.

We are in the doorway of the former coffee shop beneath my apartment. Behind me, stenciled in black script across the glass door, is the name of the place, EXPRESSO, which was supposed to mean that you could get your espresso quickly, but only half of that message got to the people of the town since they all pronounced the drink "expresso" anyway. There were lots of good reasons why the place closed.

"You actually won?" Pauly asks.

I'm standing with one hand in my pocket. The other hand is open flat up, the ticket in my hand. "I actually did. Fifty bucks. Got two of the numbers. Exact order." I shrug. "Guess I gotta take half the town to King's now."

"What, Adam? That doesn't mean anything. He just says that. I think there's a law anyway, against the seller of the ticket demanding a kick-back."

I now shove the other hand, the one with the

ticket in it, into my pocket. I stand there with my back to the door of Expresso and a window extending out toward the street on either side of me, as if I'm speaking from deep inside a three-walled glass box.

"What the hell, Pauly. Adam didn't *demand* anything. He's probably never demanded a single thing in his life. It's just a line his dad wrote for him so he'd have something to say to the customers."

With my shoulder blades, I push myself off and start across the street to the Laundromat.

"It's the principle of the thing," Pauly says.

I have to laugh. I turn around and walk most of the way backward while talking to my buddy.

"Principle, Paul? When your cat died you put it in a *mailbox*."

"That was grief, made me do that," Pauly says, though he gets a jolt of nostalgia from the story that causes him to splutter a small laugh. "Anyway, I got her back, didn't I?"

"Just because you forgot to take her tags off, numbnuts."

He splutters again as I shove open the door to the 'mat.

"Adam," I snap.

Adam looks up calmly from feeding coins into the big stainless-steel large-capacity washer that sits at the back of the store.

"Adam, you were right. It was a winner." I hold up the ticket for him to see.

Adam Everly's nearly-white gray eyes go huge. "No!" he insists.

"Yes!" I insist.

"Maybe!" Pauly insists.

Adam breaks off in the middle of what he's doing and comes rushing toward the front. I hold the ticket out in front of him, as if Adam's coming by on his carousel horse to grab the brass ring.

But he doesn't. He sweeps right on by and heads to the counter, to the phone. Picks up and dials madly.

"So exciting, so exciting," Adam Everly buzzes.

"So exciting," I repeat, not to mock Adam, but because Adam's fever is contagious.

Pauly is immune, though. "I'll be outside," he says in a hard-boiled bored voice.

"Ya, Dad," Adam shouts into the phone. "I sold it. I sold it to him last night. First one first one I ever—" Adam stops talking, starts nodding at the phone. "How much?" he then asks me.

"Fifty."

"Fifty, Dad. Ya." Pause. "Well it is much. I think it's much."

"I think it's much," I say, loudly, leaning toward fiber-optic Asa Everly.

"He thinks it's much. Oakley thinks it's much. You know how much that is? At fifty cents a pound, I gotta do . . ."

I rush in to shore up Adam's momentum dip. "A hundred pounds."

"A hundred pounds of people's laundry, Dad. That's like a million pairs of underwear I gotta fold. And touch. Sweaty and stained and . . . even *after* they come out of the washer, Daddy . . ."

I no longer want to be here for this.

"Dad? . . . Yes, I know what time it is. I thought you would want to . . ."

The moment when Asa hangs up on Adam registers clearly on the son's face. He holds the receiver to his ear a few seconds longer. "Okay. Okay, I'll talk to you later then," he says while watching me.

We stand there staring at each other. Adam, red-faced, pops open the cash register and starts counting out the cash.

"I woke him up," Adam says to the money drawer. He is apologizing to his father and to me at the same time. "He wasn't awake yet, and the phone . . . our phone has a real screechy ring . . . he's not feeling well either. . . ."

Then he looks up from the counting.

"I d-d-d-don't have enough," he says. "M-m-m-money in the till . . ." It seems very likely that Adam Everly is going to cry. "Th-th-this after-noon, I s-s-s-swear . . ."

I hold my ground, which is exactly what I do not wish to do. I want to fly, to evaporate, to leave Adam Everly in peace, or as close to peace as he can get.

"You can bring it to King's," I say calmly, as if this is just one more guy who's come up a little short when he owes another guy. "Dinner tonight like I promised."

Hard to buck Adam up. "I think it might be

a f-f-f-federal o-f-f-fense, for me not to have your m-money."

Pauly starts banging on the window, waving me out. I start for the door, point mock-menacingly at Adam. "You're lucky," I say. "I'd drop a dime on ya . . . but you got all five hundred of my dimes."

Outside, I want a laugh now. "He didn't have my money."

Pauly's eyes bug. "Is that typical, or what? You didn't win like seventy million . . . you want me go break his legs?"

I shake my head. "Thanks anyway. But he said he'd get it this afternoon and bring it with him later. The important part though, Paul, is that he's got it by tonight, because I also get to take Lilly to dinner as well."

"My Lilly?"

"Yup. Just like Adam, she said if I win I gotta take her to King's. It's a matter of principle now." I start walking a little bit faster, so Pauly has to talk to my back.

"You don't make me jealous, y'know, Oakley. You might be the only guy in this town—you might be the only guy on *earth* who doesn't make me jealous."

"Damn," I say. But I already knew that. But that doesn't stop me from trying. "Two dates for dinner. I'll be getting all kinds of sex tonight."

"Well," Pauly says coolly, "both kinds, anyway."

*　*　*

Lilly tells me when I call that she can't make it to King's tonight. Says she's got a date.

"The rat," I say.

She laughs at that.

"He knew I was taking you . . . so cancel Pauly. Better yet, stand him up."

"Maybe it's not with Pauly," she says mysteriously.

Right. She's even acting like him. "Fine. Your loss."

"Good luck," she says, chuckles, then hangs up.

When I walk into King's I am further thrown. Adam Everly is there, fretting himself into a puddle. And sitting with him is Pauly.

"Don't you have a date?" I say to Paul as I sit down across from him. I hand my napkin immediately to Adam. He mops his brow.

"No, I don't have a date," Paul says.

"You have a date with Lilly, don't you?"

"No, I thought you had a date with Lilly."

"All right now, what's going—"

"She's baby-sitting," Pauly says. "She stood you up. Get used to it."

"I d-d-don't have your money," Adam blurts.

"Oh, friggin' spoil it, why don'tcha," Pauly snaps.

I sigh. "I'm not eating tonight, am I, guys?"

"See," Pauly says, pointing at me. "See, Oakley, there it is right there. Your constant negativity. You have no faith, no optimism. That's why you need me."

"You're the reason I'm so negative. What did you do to me now?"

"You're going to hurt my feelings any minute now, Oakley."

"He m-m-made me do it, Oakley."

"Where's my money?"

Pauly smiles. Sometimes I get the feeling my primary function is to play into his hands. "It's right in here," he says, pointing to a canvas bag at his feet. The bag is wiggling.

Chellie King comes over to serve us. She's a bit of a relief. Chellie King is an endlessly optimistic person, nearly positive spirited enough to offset my attitude.

"You guys ready to order?" she asks, pencil poised.

"Go away, Chellie," I say. "I'm gonna kill somebody."

"Why is that bag moving?" she asks.

"D-d-don't kill me, Oakley."

Chellie King peeks into the bag. "Ugh! Pauly, you are so freaking weird. That is a health code violation." She grabs Pauly by the shirt and pulls him out of his chair. "You and your bag of rats get the hell out of here."

"I'm sorry," Adam Everly pleads. "I'm sorry, Chellie. I'm sorry, Oakley."

Pauly is laughing.

I speak with exaggerated calm, the way you do when you're going insane. "You spent my fifty bucks on a bag of rats?"

This only makes him laugh harder. "It's

not rats. It's only one rat."

Chellie King is shoving him with both hands, out the door.

Adam Everly and I follow him. The only possible explanation is morbid curiosity.

"You're going to thank me for this eventually," Paul says, backing away from me.

I am not going to thank him. "Ever wonder what it would feel like to have a fifty-dollar rat up your ass?"

"Been there, done that," he says just before I snag the bag.

I am staring into it. "It is. It's an actual rat."

"Not just any rat," Pauly says. "A thoroughbred."

"Ya, Oakley," Adam Everly says.

"Okay, here's the thing," Pauly explains as I stick the bag back in his hands. He scoops the little creature out and cradles it. It is not all that little actually. It is big, and white. It is fat. It has a big rear end. "He's a racing rat."

I turn and start walking away.

Pauly grabs me. "Listen. I knew a guy . . . he was cash strapped, and he had this rat. They race them on the circuit, you know, all through the six counties. Anyway, this is the famous White Rabbit."

He's looking at me like he's just introduced me to Babe Ruth.

"I'll d-d-do your laundry for free, Oakley, for, like, a year. I'm sorry. . . ."

"Sure you've heard of the White Rabbit. Son

of the Galloping Ghost and the Silver Fox?"

I am staring at him as hard as I can, but if anyone was ever immune to the power of staring, it's Pauly. "Fifty bucks," I say. "For a racing rat. For a fat racing rat."

"Don't be a dope, Oakley. For bloodlines like he's got? Plus your license . . . he's got papers, you know . . . and his colors. . . ." Pauly holds up some tiny emerald-colored racing silks with the number thirteen on them. "It was a steal, really."

"Good word there, Paul. How much of my money is left?"

"You owe me fifteen."

My mouth drops open. I look to Adam Everly.

"K-k-kicked in fifteen myself."

Pauly's beaming as he tucks our little athlete and all his gear back into the bag. "Fine, you don't have to pay me back. We're all investors. We're a syndicate."

Morbid curiosity. Again. How much of my life has been driven by nothing more than morbid curiosity? Before I know it, we are at . . . the track. It is a barn about twenty-five miles north, off Route 95. There are grizzled old Yankee types scattered all over the place, putting *their* little investments through their paces. Rodents running wind sprints all over the place.

"The *buzz* of this joint," Pauly says. "Don't you love sports?"

"Why, Pauly? Please, why are you doing this to me?"

"Because, Oakley, because I am the only person who really cares about you. See, you were going to take that fifty bucks and do what? You were going to eat some crap food, have some boring conversation just like every conversation you try to have without me, then you'd finish up by having sex with my girlfriend and Adam Everly."

"What?" Adam says. "What?" He is having trouble prioritizing. Should he be more freaked about all the rats all over the floor, or about having sex with me?

"But," says Pauly, "instead you have Pauly. Thinking-about-you-all-the-time Pauly. And I know all about your disturbing lack of ambition, and I am determined not to let you rot in your own inertia. You need a catapult, something to propel you into bigger and better things."

"Bigger and better?"

"Hey, listen. I tried to get you a racehorse, but none of the available fifty-dollar stallions seemed likely to win much. With White Rabbit, though, you can make your money back *tonight*, and go on to earn lots more. Stop laughing, Oakley, I'm serious."

You know, he is. He is deadly serious.

"Ahh," Adam yelps, running a quick small circle. "A damn rat just ran over my f-f-foot."

"So what," Pauly says. "These are all clean celebrity rats."

"This was not a racing rat."

"Ah, well, probably just a groupie then."

It is getting so that I am having to work hard at remaining angry. "How often do they do this stupidity?"

"Three nights a week, and what, are you afraid this stupidity is going to cut into your going to the Laundromat to watch strangers fold their undies?"

"I suppose you may have a point in there someplace."

"Now you're thinking. And remember this—when his racing days are over, there's still serious money to be made in stud fees."

I have to laugh. This, finally, is what I am aspiring to. "Ah, my ticket to the bigs. Pimping for rats." And the laugh feels good. The laugh alone may have been worth the fifty bucks. "Not that I'm gonna take this seriously," I say, "but just for the laugh, how much can we win?"

"Five bucks to enter, twelve rats, winner take all. Sixty clams per race."

"Th-th-that's why I did it, Oakley," Adam Everly says. "The upside . . . the upside, it's really high. We could, you know, really do well . . . show people, show people we can do something, we can win something, we can make, like, s-s-s-something. . . ."

Poor Adam Everly is getting all frothy. Poor Adam Everly wants to show his dad he can manage a champion rat racer.

A small portable stereo plays the silly bugle call that they do at the beginning of horse races. This is soooo stupid. I am relieved that nobody I know can see me here. Then I look over to my syndicate-mates, pep-talking White Rabbit. I'm glad no sane people I know can see me.

But as he lines up in lane three, I have butterflies in my stomach.

What the hell am I doing with butterflies in my stomach?

"I got butterflies," Adam Everly says.

"I got flippin' butterfuckinflies in my stomach," Pauly says.

And why not? Why couldn't we make something out of this? It *is* better than watching laundry tumble. Just because it is a patently Pauly idea doesn't mean it can't bear fruit.

"You fired up?" Pauly asks me, bumping up against me as we hang over the rail of the oval tabletop track.

"I am," I say. Then I notice, "So is he."

White Rabbit is acting the fool among his peers. As they await the start, all the other competitors are doing ordinary rodent things, licking their little hands, slicking back their hair, shitting. But our boy is going off the charts, doing like, back flips and handstands, chasing his tail and trying to eat the AstroTurf carpeting of the track. "What's his problem?" I ask. "I thought he was a pro at this."

Pauly looks a tad nervous as well. "Ah, he'll be fine. He's just a little excited . . . 'cause you're here watching."

I shove him away. Then the gun goes off, and so do the rats.

The first lap of the oval goes very well, as White Rabbit is off like a bullet. There's nobody close to him. I cannot believe the noise level in the barn, like the Indy 500 is going off here. Coming into the second lap, White Rabbit is creaming the field, and I'm thinking, My god what a rush. Pauly was right. This rat is a thoroughbred. This might really be something. I turn to my mates. Pauly is whooping like a madman. Adam Everly is biting his lip, looking more like an expectant father than a fractional owner of a racing rat. I can't stop nervous goofy laughing.

Until the event. All White Rabbit needs to do is cruise through those last three laps, collect the food bits that have been sprinkled in front of him, and then we'll take him out for champagne. But he goes haywire.

First he reverses. Goes back where he came from. Stops. Starts jumping into the air. High into the air. On his third jump, he goes over the barrier and lands in lane four, where he comes face-to-face with his nearest competitor.

Whom he attacks, with as much fury as he can muster. And he can muster plenty. It is a pretty ugly sight, as White Rabbit turns out to be just as good a mauling rat as he was a running rat.

My stomach fills again, with something not at all like butterflies. As White Rabbit, son of Gray Ghost and Silver Fox, puts his opponent to merciless death. And then proceeds to eat him.

We watch in silent horror. Until the official—
that is, the guy with the air rifle—comes out and
ends the carnage with one quick shot.

White Rabbit appears not to care much
either way. He dies with a bloody smile on his
face.

Adam Everly is inconsolable. He rides in the
bed of the truck with his head in his hands right
up to his front door.

"I still owe you a dinner," I say, hoping he
takes it as a joke.

"I still owe you the money," he says. No
joke.

Pauly swings the truck around to drop me
off.

"I feel bad," he says.

"C'mon, Pauly," I say.

"No, like, really bad. This was serious. You
mighta thought it was a goof, but I thought it
was no goof. I was thinking we coulda been onto
something here. I worry about you, y'know."

That line is a showstopper. I make a small
gurgle before managing actual speech.

"You. Worry. About me."

"No kidding, Oak. I wonder where you'll be,
what you'll do. If I'm ever not around to keep
you going."

"I was a *little* depressed before. Now shit,
Pauly, what am I, Adam Everly, you gotta set me
up in the family rat business before you croak?"

He's parked in front of the coffee shop now,

beneath my front window, which is a few feet from where my dad is probably sleeping.

"No," he says, jamming the truck into park and facing me, ultraserious. "Difference between you and Adam is you got plenty on the ball, but no inclination to do shit with it. Difference between me and Asa is I *love* my boy."

I open the truck door and get ready to bolt. He makes it so hard on me, when I want simplicity. When I want to merely hate him or pity him or fear him or fume at him. I need to be physically removed from him to acomplish any of that, or he does this to me.

"Anyway," he says, "I'm sorry how it turned out."

"Ah, there'll be other brainless schemes."

"That's the spirit, Oakley boy."

"And besides, it wasn't you who jumped the fence and ate the opponent."

He stares at the brake pedal. "But it was me fed him six No-Doz."

I stare at the sky. I could kill him finally. I could, I could, I will.

I won't, of course.

"I'm going to see Lilly," he offers. "Wanna come?"

I continue to stare at the sky, but I'm just being dramatic, because I'm out of ideas.

"The laundry's closed," he says, with the same Pauly enthusiasm that he invests in all his nonsense, "but we could find who's hung out their washing today and go watch it dry on the line."

I climb back into the truck. "That's the spirit," I say. We speed off to get Lilly, as if time were an issue.

# In Spite of Myself

Mostly
as I lie
sandwiched
between days
sandwiched
between needy sheets
despite the Laundromat
being right there
I wonder
how they do it.
Why they do it.
Does anybody else
ever feel
like lying down

and staying down?
Hamstrung.
By mania
by loneliness
by family
by friends.
Nobody quits.
From what I can see.
Nobody quits.
Would god not smile
on nobody quits?
Why does god not smile
on nobody quits?
Why does god not smile?

And why should I be
a home team fan.
Despite history
despite intelligence
despite common
sense.
I root.
Despite myself.
I do this much
in spite of myself.
I pray.

In spite of myself
when nobody is watching
I pray.
I look
from my window
across the street
down the street
at the spire
and I aspire
and I swear
I'd take a flyer
on the white god rocket
for the one smallest sign.
In spite of myself
I pray for the gleam gap-toothed smile.
The sign.
That god is
worthy
of the guy
who thinks
my underwear
is sacred
worthy
of the pale rodent
with the good heart
and the bad wiring.

Or does the business of being god
make him too weary
to bother
to smile
at his own
stammering
glory?

# CAFÉ SOCIETY

I WALK ALONG, TOWARD the stop where the ancient yellow bus would pick me up and do its best to take me to the regional technical high school twelve miles away. There is only a handful of kids from this area going to the Tech, so we don't get the prime service. The bus is cold, especially in the mornings, and seems even colder the way the students are spread out front to back, six benches between pairs or individuals. The hills are tough too, even for a healthy vehicle, and the groaning of the old yellow Bluebird would quash any conversation, so mostly nobody tries. By the time we get to school, even doing nothing seems like too much effort. We each take our own window seat, hug ourselves against the cold, and stare off into the hills.

Pauly would make the trip a little more lively, but mostly that's not possible. He's technically in

176

the Tech, but not really. Sometimes he'll go on a Tuesday, when they're serving bacon burgers for lunch.

I have the time. I head to King's, where I can tank up with something good and hot. And absorb some Chellie King.

I sit at a small circular table, small circular tables being one of the two options with big rectangular ones being the other. It is a fairly large place, larger than it needs to be, since it's actually a converted movie theater, which used to hold probably a hundred people. The floor is even sloped ever so slightly, so that when you walk into the place gravity directs diners down to the back, and that is how tables fill in King's naturally, back to front. The windows are small and the lights are always low, as if the feature is perpetually about to begin. SEAT YOURSELF, the sign-on-a-stand reads, as if you really have any say in the matter.

"I am so glad you're here," Chellie says excitedly. Chellie, short for Michelle. It's all spelled out on her name tag, in tiny print. And though I like to be a gentleman and though I know her name perfectly well by now, I cannot break the habit of staring at her name tag. Chellie King has what is generally referred to as a womanly figure, to go with her little delicate hands and kind of youngish face and singsongy voice. Makes more the miracle that she's got the ego of a much uglier person.

"Hey, Chelle," I say.

"Hey. Listen, you have to come back on Saturday."

"But I'm thirsty *now*," I say.

"Now *and* Saturday," she says, like she's in a big hurry to go someplace, even though she works here day and night four days wrapped around her classes. Another of Whitechurch's family-run businesses.

"Jeez, Chelle," I joke. "I mean, I know I'm renowned for not doing *much* with myself, but I think I can do better than *that*. And twice in one week?" I try to sound pained. "I could die from that."

She starts writing. "So you eat the donuts. They're imported. Can't hurt you." As she finishes dictating my order to herself, she scurries back to the kitchen, where both of her parents are waiting to fill the order of one donut and one coffee/cocoa combo. There is no one else in the restaurant.

"So you know how I'm up at the junior college, right?" Chellie asks, plunking herself down along with the order. "And how I'm studying in the hotel-and-restaurant-management program?"

I look, I suppose, blankly.

"Oh sure, you knew that. Well anyway, after like begging and crying, and sug*gest*ing till I am royal *blue* in the face, my folks have finally consented to hand the whole place over. To me!"

"Chellie!" I say, jumping up out of the chair when she does. But I am truly happy for Chellie. She has tried just about everything the junior college has to offer. Public-speaking courses. Computer-Aided Design. Fashion Design. Computer-Aided Interior Design. German. Until she finally decided that the family dynasty was the way to go.

But no one ever expected her parents to hand it over while they were still alive.

"This is amazing," I say as we take our seats again. "So, what, your folks finally decide to take the Florida option?"

"What? Oh no. Don't be simple, Oakley. They're letting me have Saturday night. Just. Come on, you know my old man. He says he spent his whole life working his butt off to get this place, and if he wants to spend the rest of his years poisoning the good people of Whitechurch, then that's his right.

"And it is," she adds graciously.

"Well sure, it is," I say, swallowing a big blueberry bite of donut. "So what do you get, exactly?"

Here she gets even further lathered up, grabbing my drink and taking a long calming gulp. She speaks with a mocha mustache. A lovely mustache. She endures it patiently and doesn't flinch when I reach up and dab at her lip with my napkin.

"I make it mine," Chellie says when I finish. "I take *over*. Give this place some *style*. 'Cause let's face it, my parents are the sweetest folks on earth, but their idea of taste is hand-painted zebra T-shirts. Ready for the concept? Café Cinema.

Right? I'm gonna open up that moldy thing." She points to the back of the room, where the old Rialto curtain hangs, floor to ceiling, gold satin with diagonal maroon stripes. "And I'm going to show a classic old movie, just like in the old days, only with table service. Classy stuff. Little sandwiches and guacamole I'm going to make myself. Martha Stewart shit all over the place."

Chellie King and her endless, inventive plans. You can't help but be a fan. I can't anyway. "Beats hell outta racing rats, Chelle," I say.

"What?" she asks.

The bus comes gasping to a halt in front of King's, and the driver looks in the window. His name is Alekos and he only speaks Greek, but he knows where to find every student, as if he creeps along peeking in every window of the town, rounding 'em up without ever dismounting.

"Gotta go, Chellie," I say, standing.

Chellie scootches up and kisses me on the mouth. A blast furnace of a kiss from a friend, and my day, so early, has already reached far higher than most of my days.

So even I can stumble across a great idea now and then. Coming to Chellie King was my great idea of the day.

Saturday comes cool, ideal autumn, crisp so you have to walk a little faster, hug yourself, hunch your shoulders so a downdraft can't sneak into you. But not so cold you'd rather be indoors unless you have a good reason.

And enough of Whitechurch has been convinced that Café Cinema is a good reason that the place is nearly three-quarters full and buzzing with noise. I, however, have no date, unless you count Adam Everly, whom I do not count because someone who owes you money makes for a lousy date. Lilly said the same thing she said the other night—she had a date, and maybe not with Pauly, and no I didn't need to be sticking my nose in. Then my other steady, Pauly, was AWOL when I went looking, meaning he's either out with her or stalking her. Just another night with Whitechurch's First Couple.

But signs are good that I won't even miss them. King's big old curve-top Magnavox radio is patched into the movie sound system, which makes it only slightly buzzier than it usually sounds. The local station is playing its regular Saturday-night oldies show. There is a popcorn smell, but it's beginning to be overpowered by a deep-fryer smell.

"Oakley, Oakley, Oakley," Chellie says as she greets me at the door, and I feel like VIP-BMOC all at once. If this is what she's doing to every customer, she will be one of the great entrepreneurs and won't be waiting nobody's tables for long. She's half whispering because she is, after all, the proprietor here tonight, and doesn't want to come off all silly-sounding, especially dressed like she is.

"Wow, Chelle," I say, and can barely manage to say it.

"Ya?" she asks, taking a step back for me to admire her. She spins. Stops.

"Oh ya. Wow. Pow, even."

It is undeniable, anyway. Chellie is wearing a floor-length rust-colored velvet dress, cut discreetly, yet unmistakably, to the exact shape of Chellie. With a very low neckline.

"Good." She grabs my arm and yanks hard, as if she's ringing a great bell somewhere. "Good, good, good. I drove down to Boston to get this. Convinced my dad it was an investment. Cost six times what I'll probably take in tonight, but look." She rushes the length of the room, down the sloping floor, all the way to the foot of the stage where, coolly now, she strokes the thick, heavy, lush fabric of the stage curtain, which closely matches her dress.

She rushes back to me. "See," she says, "it's so I have some clear, obvious connection to the theater. Like you can *tell* it's mine. You can tell, right, Oakley, that this is mine, right when you walk in?"

I look all around, checking out the crowd. "Everybody here knew it was yours before they even laid eyes on the dress, Chelle. But now they also know you're the queen. That dress is the most elegant thing Whitechurch ever saw."

Chelle drops her head slightly, like she's checking out the cleavage like everybody else.

"I look like a fool, don't I, Oakley? This is too much. This is stupid."

No, no, no. Ever hear something so wrong—not wrong as in incorrect, but wrong as in cosmically *not right*—that it hurt you to hear it? I could doubt the plan, but I could not doubt Chellie King.

"Chelle, don't run out of gas now. You gotta make this thing fly. This is the most excitement I've had since my rat died."

She looks up again. "What's with this rat theme lately, Oakley?"

"Not important. The important thing is no guts, no glory. Get your velvety self in gear and show this burgh a little class."

She brightens. "I'd love to make, you know, a little statement. Not a big deal or anything—"

"Too late, you're already a big deal. You going to show me to my table so I can start getting fresh with the hostess, or can I just start here?"

She begins, with a slightly exaggerated but not much exaggerated swingy sexy walk, to show me to my reserved table. When we get there, she leans in and says, "Damn, I wish you were a few years older."

"I brought a fake ID," I answer, as I sit.

"Keep it handy," she says, squeezes my shoulder, and off she goes to make the rest of the crowd half as happy.

"Oak. Oak. Oak," Adam Everly says, and it sounds like the nervous yap of a little dog. He's sitting, his hands folded tightly on the table in front of him, and he's rigid. "Oak, Oak."

I can't help but laugh. "What's with the barking, Adam?"

This Adam Everly takes as his cue to stand, just as rigidly as he was sitting. "Gotta talk to ya, Oak." He makes a motion with his head the way only the old-movie hard guys of fifty years ago did, and I get up to follow Adam down front, up against the stage where nobody sits.

"What's wrong?" I ask, but can't manage to get too worked up about it. While I'm talking to Adam he's actually staring straight up, at the massive expanse of curtain that obscures the screen.

"Jeez, Chellie coulda made herself five hundred dresses out of this thing." He reaches out to feel the fabric, rubs it between his thumb and middle finger. Rust velvet dust twinkles to the floor.

"I d-d-d-don't . . ."

Adam's stutter is worse than ever. He is so frustrated he stops completely. I study his face and can see some kind of calculations, a mantra, a pep talk, something going on inside Adam that might get him through this.

"Don't *have* it," he blurts finally. "D-don't *have* your money. Oakley. Not all of it at least."

"What?" I'm more surprised than anything, but I shouldn't be, should I? "What, Adam, haven't we been over this already?"

"No, no, you d-d-don't understand. I g-got your money. F-from my savings, and what I got outta people's pockets . . ."

"Adam!" I say, mock-horrified.

"Only when I'm desperate," he says. "But then, anyway, I was all s-s-set to pay you back, 'cause the rat wasn't really a payback in the end . . . b-b-b-b-b-b-b-but it's all gone away again. . . ."

"Adam, what is it now, you got a gambling problem? Drugs? What?" I chuckle as I say this because Adam Everly is the man who would never have any of those problems. The unseemly problems. The character problems. Adam has his hands full with all of life's other problems.

He stares at the floor, clenches his fists. Walks in place, like he's doing a little fox-trot there by himself.

"No, I got a n-n-numbnuts problem. I was t-trying to do something smart. Something smart. Bought some soap. Some cheap s-s-soap p-p-p-*powder*." He stamps his boot at the memory. "Thought I was smart. Thought I was makin' a *move*, Oakley. Thought this was the score for sure. From this guy who came in . . . real cheap . . . increase our margin on the laundering . . . thirty b-b-b-bucks . . . shit made about as much suds as a b-b-b-box of sh-sh-sh-sh-*sugar*."

"Oh" is all I can say. Which is not quite enough to make Adam Everly shake his guilt. He hands me a twenty-dollar bill. Then he smacks himself on the side of his head with the heel of that same hand.

I grab his wrist as he's about to do it again.

Only then does Adam look at me.

"That's really stupid, Adam. Don't do that." There is a hardness in my voice that I hadn't planned. His regular stupidity, the stupidity I like, of rats and sudsless suds and all that, that's the stuff I can bear. That is different. "It's not that much money. Don't hit yourself over my money. Just don't do that, all right? I'll hit you myself if I feel that bad about it, then we'll both feel better."

This, for whatever reason, calms Adam Everly. "I won't eat nothin'," he says with a small smile and no stutter. "And I'll just have water." He leads the way back up the slope toward our table. "You don't have to worry about takin' me to dinner. We'll call that even."

"Even my ass," I say, giving him a small shove in the back. "You are washing my socks for fuckin' *ever*."

We take our seats again, and Chellie comes sailing over to the table. "I got a job for somebody," she says, waving a cordless phone.

Adam grabs the phone eagerly, anxious, I suppose, to start paying down that mounting karmic debt.

"Okay," she says, "you just keep hitting Redial. And when the radio-station guy answers, tell him you want to hear 'Saturday Night at the Movies' by the Drifters."

Chellie does not wait for acknowledgment from Adam Everly before turning away. Now that is optimism.

"Chelle, Chelle," I say, bringing her back. "Where are your folks? They helping you out?"

Chellie beams. "No way. They cleared out to give me the whole place to win or lose on my own. Kind of special too, their first Saturday night off in years, so my dad said they were going on a date."

"Sweet," I say.

"Damn sweet," Chellie says and bolts off to take an order from a bunch of noisy kids from the junior college who have come and filled three of the big long rectangular tables against one wall. Two of the other part-time waitresses are helping out, but Chellie is still twelve times busier than she ever was in here before. The difference is she's the boss. And she's in that dress. And she can't get the smile off her face. I swear I can smell smells that couldn't be on the menu. Fried clams, sausage, peppers, onions, and pot roast. Whatever song buzzes over the radio, whether it's "Misty," or "I Fought the Law and the Law Won," is somebody's special tune, and inspires a singalong.

Adam Everly is scrunched way down in his chair, dialing numbers on Chellie's cordless, covering his free ear with his hand, wincing with concentration amid the katzenjammer of Chellie King's little masterpiece of an evening. The squawkie radio is playing "Roll Over, Beethoven" now, so still we have not gotten through.

"Just hit the redial, Adam," I say. I cannot take the job over or he'll be devastated, so I act strictly in a support role. "Would you like a drink?"

"W-water's fine," Adam says quietly. "What's the movie, anyway?"

This was the tightly held secret of the week. Not only what the movie would be, but where it would come from and how Chellie would run it. Nobody seemed to recall when the Rialto last screened anything, and the inner workings of the place were a complete mystery. Chellie would give out nothing but buzzwords in advance. It would be old, it would be classic and classy and golden age. An event. A throwback. A happening. A moment.

"When's The Moment, Chelle?" I call out over the laughter of the college kids and the crackly croak of Elvis Presley singing "Teddy Bear."

"Order something, ya stiff," she calls back, which hardly seems like an answer although, ya, I suppose it is.

I pick up a hand-lettered—neatly and lovingly and almost calligraphy hand-lettered—menu. I read it up one side, past the salmon paté sandwiches and tandoori chicken roll-ups and falafel and vinegar mussels, and down the other, past profiteroles and banana fritters and baked cheese and cinnamon-yogurt apples. There is no pot roast, but I don't quite feel like complaining.

"Yes!" Adam Everly shouts, shutting the phone off and slapping his palms loudly on the table.

"Now what's up?" I ask.

He says nothing, but raises one hand and extends a pointer finger. He's pointing at the air, at the air*waves*. Adam Everly is beaming with . . . is that pride I see?

*And this very special special request goes out to Michelle King, the Queen. Proprietress of the newest, gotta-get-there night place in the kingdom . . .*

Everybody claps and hollers as Chellie, in her fine dress, balancing a tray of full-pint full-strength ciders over her head, weaves blushing among the tables while the Drifters sing down on her, *Wellll, Saturday night at eight o'clock/ I know where I'm gonna go. . . .*

"What a goofy song," somebody says, laughing, singing along.

"What a party," one of the college guys says, raising a glass to Chellie.

Everyone in the room does likewise, toasting and cheering Chellie while she stands there, blushing, beaming, bursting, *winning. . . .*

There is now a great racket, a clattering, coming from the projection room. Rather, from the small rectangular openings high on the wall of the projection room.

The crowd is clapping and vocal again, at the first signs of cinema life. Like in a haunted theater, small flickering lights, clicks and clacks of sound magically spill out of the rectangles even though nobody has seen anyone go up there. There isn't even a visible entrance.

Chellie is as stunned as everybody else. I take my opportunity.

"I think I need to tell you something." I start mumbling an explanation.

"You don't have *what*?" Chellie asks me.

Adam Everly slinks down in his seat, then quickly sits back up. "Oh boy," he says, because the movie is starting.

The line-slashed black-and-white figures begin to play on the big curtain, which is reluctant to open. A couple of patrons get up to help, each pulling gently but steadily on one decaying sheet of dusty curtain, towing it to the wings. By the time the screen is clear, Moe is already slapping Larry on the broad bald middle of his head.

Everybody is clapping. Everybody is happy. It's the Three Stooges, and that can't miss. Chellie is watching the people, her people in her place, as they enjoy themselves. Chellie claps, she claps for that. She smiles, covers her mouth, claps again like a child, or like an insanely proud stage mother. This is all hers, and it's sweet now.

The Stooges are in form too. They're testifying at a murder trial, telling everybody who killed Cock Robin. Rhyming and rapping and doing this cockeyed film-noir foolishness. Fine foolishness. Curly is madness. He is genius.

Adam Everly may have laughed this hard at some point in his life, but I wouldn't bet on it.

All of the jumping night side of Whitechurch—which, with the Chinese restaurant closed, means everybody at Café Cinema—is in agreement. This is the funniest film in the slickest cabaret serving the funkiest tandoori . . . just the best of everything. Chellie wins.

Then the Stooges solve Cock Robin, but we won't give it away.

The social whirl of Whitechurch pauses while whoever it is changes reels. More ciders, more food, more good things for Chellie, more IOU from me. Even the reel changing is interesting, though. Who the hell ever gets to see reel changing? Numbers, bubbles of oil, slashes across the white of the screen. If there was a rock-and-roll band standing in front of that show it would be a brilliant backdrop. And since rock and roll doesn't stop in Whitechurch, this is *it*.

Funny, how something so small and silly as this, something concocted by a regular, determined and unreasonably hopeful small-town dreamer girl from the CC, funny, how something like that can suddenly change the everything of a town, making it livable and likable and worth your time.

"You're the queen, Chellie King," I call as she scoots from one happy table to another. She immediately bees it my way. "Hot damn, you did it, Michelle," I say right up close to her because she's right up close to me. I use the full-name Michelle, which nobody much says. And like the Beatles said it too. Mee-chelle. Ma Belle. "What's Ma Belle anyway?" I ask, to make it academic, to make it less dangerous, because I'm scaring myself a bit, and because the sound of Mee-chelle

Ma Belle is suddenly the most heart-twisting
sequence I ever heard.

"Means my place or yours," Chellie says, not
helping me out much.

"Shush!" Adam yelps, shocking everyone
into doing just that. Adam saying shush is like
Pauly saying I love you to somebody besides me.
Uncharted islands, those. "The next one's starting."

Adam Everly's mighty roar is plowed over by
the MGM lion's, and the screechy, blarey trum-
pets of the opening of the movie, volume way too
loud and sounding like it's being played inside an
oil drum.

Everybody is clapping enthusiastically,
though no one knows yet what the film is.

But they know Frank Sinatra is in it.

And now they know Kim Novak is in it.

And Darren McGavin.

"What's *The Man with the Golden Arm*?"
one of the college boys calls out.

"Shit, it's James Bond," another one answers,
and they high-five and knock foreheads.

Adam Everly leans over the table. It's hard to
see now because the lights are way low, unlike
for the Three Stooges, who did not rate dim
lighting because they are not art. "I didn't know
Sinatra played Bond."

Chellie, who is standing, like a sentry in the
middle of the room, must be beaming in on every
conversation. She answers both tables. "Sinatra's
a musician, dummy. It's about heroin."

"Whoa!" the college boys call. "Like *Trainspotting*. Cool."

Adam Everly is cautious, wading into the conversation. He's concentrating on the credits. "That can't be, Chelle. They didn't have heroin yet in the fifties. And even if they did, Frank never would have touched it."

"Shut *up*, will you!" And the speaker isn't me, isn't one of the college guys, isn't even Chellie, who would have every right to be saying it. The voice comes down from the projection booth.

Nestor. That explains much. Nestor, and the Rialto, have their very own homemade book in the library, where Ophelia Lennon keeps it on display in a glass case, and if you are a close personal friend of hers, you may leaf through it carefully.

Nestor owned the theater when it was a theater. He ran it when it truly was the center of social life for all Whitechurch, and for several smaller towns beyond, if you can imagine smaller towns beyond. When Nestor would run *Ben Hur* or *The Public Enemy* or *The Hound of the Baskervilles* in his Ajax-clean theater, back when those curtains were new velvet an inch thick and throwing no dust, you had to get to the theater early on a Saturday Night at the Movies or boy you would be going *home* early, apologizing to your date. Little brass lanterns popping straight out from the walls lined both sides of the main hall and practically went on throwing light after they were shut off, that was how much Nestor polished them. You couldn't drop one kernel of popcorn on Nestor's floor during the show without it seeming that he was crawling under your seat to grab it up so the next crowd didn't have to put up with nobody's filth.

He loved movies, introduced movies himself from up on his stage. And he bought the movies. Word was that bachelor Nestor spent almost every dime he made from the fifties to the eighties collecting the prints of films he played. He didn't spend anything on dates, he said, because his whole life was a date. I met him one time in the library, when I was looking at his book. He sat down next to me, flipped it back to the beginning, and we leafed through it together. He never said a thing to me.

"Jeez," I say, "I guess this really is an important film, if god himself tells you to shut up."

For a while, everybody is cool and into it. Darren McGavin is creepy. Kim Novak is sweet. And as for Sinatra, he may not look like a contemporary Hollywood heroin casualty, but he sure convinces you that *something* is bothering the crap out of him, and that's good enough. For a while.

But the Whitechurch Film Festival Jury is not very tolerant. They'd really prefer *Trainspotting*.

"Choose whiskey," one of the guys yells at celluloid Frank, as if he didn't have enough problems already. "Choose the Mafia. Choose the toupee. Choose to sing 'My Way' fifty million times—"

"Choose to shut the hell up," Nestor's voice booms, and immediately you can feel the change in atmosphere.

I try to remember the last time I actually saw something worth getting into a fight about. Nothing comes to mind. Lots of nothing comes to mind, and this moment fits right in.

On the screen, Kim Novak soldiers on, desperately trying to talk to deranged Sinatra through his apartment door.

Off the screen, Chellie King is standing next to me, practically emitting sparks, as she wills the crowd to love a movie they are not going to love.

"Put the Stooges back on," one of the college guys says, and the way he says it sure sounds as if bar service has not been discontinued at that table.

"Th-th-that sounds like a g-g-good—"

"The Stooges *are* on," I say. This is bothering me suddenly. This is bothering me *so* much that I have trouble understanding it myself. I'm grinding my teeth because I did not see it coming. Being small, that's okay. I know small. I do small. I live small, and that's fine. Pathetic is not. Stupid things happen, and good ideas fail. That's routine. It's the way you react that proves whether or not you're a schmuck.

It occurs to me that, for all my lack of action, I am not a patient individual.

"We-want-the-Stooges!" comes an anonymous call from somewhere.

And I am surrounded by schmucks.

"We-want-*Trainspotting*!" comes the response from the other side of the room.

"We-want-cider!" add the college guys, laughing louder than required.

"Quiet over there, we're trying to hear the shitty movie," another schmuck says.

Then, Adam Everly does what I should be doing, if I was the kind of person who did things.

Adam Everly stands. "Should we beat them up?" he says, very grimly.

It is a pathetic moment, but more beautiful than most. Adam Everly, god love him, couldn't beat up old Nestor if it came down to that.

The lights go up before Adam Everly gets tough. Nestor is screaming up in the booth, and doing some kind of violent thrashing around. The image on the screen looks crazed, first there, then sped up, slowed, stopped, torn away. I jump to my feet.

"That is *it*!" Chellie yells. "We are closed now. Show is over!"

"That is right!" Nestor yells. He is standing at the back of the theater, the front of the restaurant, which is what it will be from now on. Nestor is in his eighties, bent over to about five feet tall. He's got uncombed, weirdly yellow hair that grows on the sides but is also dragged across the glistening top of his head. "I knew I shouldn't have done this. You are too ignorant. You young people, this *town*. Too stupid. Don't deserve my fine films. Don't understand nothing unless people are cursing and fucking all over the place. Should have burned my theater like I wanted to. It doesn't deserve this. Get out now. Get out!"

Nestor appears to have forgotten that he doesn't own the theater anymore. When nobody responds, nobody speaks or moves, he clutches his big tin film canister that looks like he could be carrying a bicycle tire inside, pulls it tight to his chest. He turns and storms off, but with his bad leg only half of him is up to storming, while the other side drags along behind.

I take a step to follow him, because now this seems important to me. I want to say something, something maybe like I like old movies, Nestor, or Remember me and you and your book and the library, Nestor? But I hear myself. I hear how it sounds. Nestor would probably clock me with the big canned *Man with the Golden Arm*.

He has managed to freeze time though, Nestor, even if he's frozen it less than he'd like. The college guys are collecting their gear and pulling out. The other unsatisfied filmgoers are taking advantage of the diversion to slip away, with only small mutters of "Thanks," and "Night, Chellie" as they scramble to find some-place that is still selling cider.

Chellie King does not seem sorry to see peo-ple go. She is all business as she starts collecting glasses and dishes off a table. Until tears slalom down her face, drop to her chest, disappear into her magnificent velvet dress that almost matches her sad old crumbly theater. The curtain will now smell like tandoori forever. She looks up, comes to her friends' table and tells them to beat it.

"We should help," Adam Everly says.

"Course we're going to help," I say.

Chellie reaches out and squeezes my forearm. "Go away. I want everybody to just be gone."

I look down at my arm where she has squeezed me. "Oh, ya, that was pretty intimidating. Guess I'll run away now. How 'bout you, Adam, you scared yet?"

"I'm gonna g-g-go hide in the kitchen," he says. He smiles big, pleased at his successful rare shot at humor. "I didn't really need to stutter that time, Chellie. I f-f-f-faked it for you."

Chellie covers her face with her hands, but peeks over the fingertips. Her eyes are smiling, and still weepy.

Adam Everly disappears into the kitchen to work on his specialty, cleaning things. A dish shatters. "I got it," he calls. "Don't worry there, I g-g-got it under control."

Chellie drops her chin to her chest in exasperation. She starts laughing for real now.

"You don't have to do this, guys," Chellie says. "It's my mess, not yours."

There's another smash in the kitchen. "It's all right," Adam calls. "I got that."

I make a dramatic sweeping gesture toward the kitchen. Then I continue around, covering the theater, the front door, and Whitechurch beyond. "It's *our* mess. Don't worry about it, this'll be fun. It's *gotta* be more fun than the movie was anyway."

Chellie goes and locks the door. She has sent her two waitresses home, but with her new assistants, the place is nearly clean by the time she picks up her broom. I take it away from her. "Go sit down," I say. "Boss don't sweep. Proprietress don't sweep. Hostess don't sweep. And anybody wearing a dress like that don't sweep."

Chellie grips the broom with both hands for a moment, while I do likewise. Then she grins, lets go, leans forward, and kisses me on the lips.

Chellie disappears into the kitchen, leaving me clutching the broom handle for support. A few minutes later she walks back into the room, which is cleaner than it has been since Nestor took care of it. She's towing a one-gallon jug of hard cider and Adam Everly. Adam is balancing a tray of pilsner glasses.

The strain is evident on his face.

"Come on, Adam," I say quietly, as if something serious is riding on this. "Come on, come on . . ."

He makes it, and this is cause for celebration.

"Come on, gentlemen," Chellie says as Adam sets down the tray of wobbling glasses. "Quittin' time."

She fills all three glasses to the top, sets them down in front of the three chairs, and the cleanup crew members sit down in front of them. We raise our glasses. The glasses hang there. What, after all, are we supposed to toast, really? Chellie had a great idea, for the wrong population. She is more certain than ever to bolt town, leaving us a hell of a lot uglier and more ignorant than we already are. We probably put the final nails in the coffin of Nestor, who only ever wanted to show his people a decent flick in a class joint, make it date night all the time, but who is probably right now sitting in the middle of a technicolor bonfire in his living room with *Wings of Desire* and *Duck Soup* and *The Great Escape* making a blue chemical flame that will eat up his drapes and himself.

Feels like something, though. Something, probably, is happening here. A toast, then.

"To White Rabbit," I say.

Chellie is a bit puzzled. "Um, the song?"

Adam Everly is not puzzled. "Is this really necessary?"

"No," I say. "Not the song. The athlete. The thoroughrat. White Rabbit, son of Gray Ghost and Silver Fox. Fastest rodent ever to wear racing silks, and not too shabby with a knife and fork, either."

"He didn't use c-c-cutlery," Adam Everly says. He starts out serious, then even he recognizes the absurdity and starts laughing. And toasting.

"I have no idea what you two are on about, but I'm thirsty."

Chellie downs fully half the glass, gasps, then speaks her piece. "See, if this would have worked, I maybe could have stayed. Y'know? Stupid town needs something. . . . Nestor's right. It's an ignorant place."

"I don't think it's a bad place," Adam Everly says softly.

Chellie dips her nose way down low to give him a hard down stare. "That's it," she says, "no more alcohol for you."

"Same old story," I say. "I'm talking about a champion. We could have brought glory to Whitechurch with White Rabbit. But it's all politics, isn't it? My rat showed just a little too much style . . . so they shot him down. Just like Kennedy. And you, Chelle."

Chellie doesn't see the comparison between our personal failures. "Shut up, Oakley. I'm serious about this. We could have, if this worked, done this a lot. It's a nice little stage up there. Isn't it a nice little stage up there?"

"That is a great dress," I say.

"It is," Adam adds, then quickly buries his nose in his drink.

"Which?" I ask. "The stage or the dress?"

Adam blushes. "The d-d-d-d-d . . ."

"Thank you," Chellie says. She reaches across and squeezes Adam's hand. "We could have done the movies, then maybe, you know, a comic, maybe a play . . . poetry nights. Can you imagine it, a nice poetry night here, a nice, like, poetry night, with wine and cheese and like, a poet, right here?"

I probably should answer. But honestly, a poetry night . . .

Chellie splutters out a laugh. "Me neither," she says.

"I keep losing Oakley's Lotto money," Adam Everly contributes.

Chellie jumps up out of her seat and dashes to the kitchen.

"Now look what you did, Adam. Your story was the one that finally broke her."

He looks worried. He looks about to run after her until she comes trotting back out carrying a bag.

"This was to be the nice finish of a nice evening," she says, handing around fortune cookies. "I was going to give one to every customer, for a laugh."

"So, it'll be the nice finish to a crap evening," I say.

"Thanks, Oakley. Hope you get the death cookie."

As we struggle with the cookies, Chellie King pounds down a whole glass of cider.

"Ignorant town," she says, "I hate this ignorant goddamn town," smashing her cookie more like a walnut. Her voice drops low, almost loses itself. "I don't want to leave it."

"What does yours say?" Adam Everly asks Chellie brightly.

"It says, 'You live in an ignorant goddamn town with the world's shittiest Chinese food.'"

Adam smiles. "I don't think it really says that, Chelle."

She relents. "'Things are looking up for you,'" she recites.

"See now," Adam Everly says. "*There's* an omen if I ever heard one."

I have just wrangled mine open. "'Things are looking up for you,'" I say, tossing the cookie fragments onto the table. "Big omen. Adam Everly, you're the last contestant."

This, apparently, is big pressure for Adam. He gets very jittery, taking a big gulp of his drink. He works the cookie open as if he wants to just bend it, not break it, so it can be reused. "'You will c-c-come into a sudden f-f-f-fortune.'" Adam pauses, rereads it, smiles, sips, sits back pleased.

I have, as I have had frequently of late, a sudden unkind spasm. I get unkind spasms even though I am not, really, unkind, and it is in fact one of the most important things to me, to be not unkind. To know that I am not. But the spasms do come, like a nervous disorder.

I reach over and snag the fortune from him. "Wait, it says 'Continued on next cookie.'" I grab another, crack it, read, "'And you will blow the fortune on a boatload of bootleg soapsuds.'"

Adam goes all righteous. He sits up proudly in his chair, sipping neatly from his drink.

"At least I try, Oakley," Adam Everly says. "And I'm not s-s-sorry, either."

Chellie King slides her chair right up next to Adam Everly's and throws an arm around him. They look at me defiantly, as if their schemes have actually *succeeded*.

They are quite a pair.

"That's the spirit," Chellie says. "If at first you don't succeed, and all that rigamarole." She stands. "I like your style, Adam Everly. You win the door prize. Take me home."

Adam Everly may yet swallow his tongue. "I, I, I, I, live the other way," he says.

She ponders that. "Well, good for you," she says. "Living that way is fine too."

Adam Everly doesn't seem to care much what she has said, as long as he is out of harm's way.

"Will *you* then?" Chellie says, walking around to my side of the table. She is leaning late-night close to me. I can feel her breath on my cheek and nothing else over any other part of me.

I don't suppose anyone is surprised when I say, "Course, Chelle. Course I'll walk you." Because most of the time "yes" is my word. Acquiesence my mode.

I help Chellie into her long wool coat. The three of us exit together quietly, walking tentatively across the room after Chellie kills all the lights. We stand on the sidewalk out front for an extra minute, looking at the breath misting out of each other.

"See that," Chellie says to Adam Everly, pointing across the street at Missus Minnever's Bed and Breakfast, which has been closed for the two years that Missus Minnever has been dead.

"I see it," Adam Everly says.

"Everybody sees it," I add. "How could you miss it? Biggest eyesore in town."

"I hear it's coming up for auction," she says, winking at Adam Everly. "Prime location. Massive possibilities, for the right syndicate . . ."

Adam Everly turns away from Ms. King, toward Missus Minnever's again, then back once more to Ms. King. He winks. I am certain it is the first time he has ever attempted this maneuver. He rubs his eye.

"We'll talk," Chellie King says. "We'll lunch on it. . . ."

I start tugging her down the sidewalk as Adam Everly waves excitedly, visions of B&B success dancing in his head.

"Well, then, good night," I say, heading off with Chellie, east. Adam Everly continues walking backward, west.

"See, this is the thing," Chellie says as she lifts my arm and wraps it like a stole around herself. She leans hard against me, so that I have to lean equally hard to keep us balanced as we walk. "The thing, the thing is . . ."

I wait, walk listen and wait. But that is it, Chellie is finished. Which is just as well. It's late. We pass the Laundromat, which is unlighted, which means nobody is fondling Whitechurch's unmentionables unless it's going on in the darkness. We pass the empty coffee shop beneath my apartment. Chellie looks up while I look straight ahead. We pass Chuck's International Auto Parts and Holly's House of Fine which is a beauty parlor and the library and the town hall and the Texaco which looks like a modern big-time gas station because Texaco forced Jason Gilmartin to build that twenty-foot-high lighted hooded island for the pumps or lose his franchise, so he built it and now it looks like Whitechurch's little piece of Vegas, screaming yellow light over the town center through the night.

We pass the burger place and the pie place and the donut place. "It's a good thing," I say, finding myself now giving Chellie a tight squeeze, then backing off, "that all these places sell only one item apiece. 'Cause if it was just one normal-size joint instead of all chopped up like this, Whitechurch would be an awfully dull place. Couldn't have *that* now, could we?"

"Christ!" Chellie roars at the thought. With the dead stop of the town this late, the sound of it rings, rolls, back west, down the main street, up the rise outbound at the far end of town. You could hear it come to a stop, *pong*, in the bell tower of First Unitarian.

We have stopped to listen to it. She smiles. She stops smiling. I do it this time. "Christ!"

We can still hear it just slightly as we walk the walk to Chellie King's sky-blue clapboard house, on the easternmost lip of the bowl that is Whitechurch. We stand on her spongy bowed rotting porch, which Mr. King will fix when he retires or when Edgar the mail carrier steps through and breaks his leg.

"My room is right there," she says, pointing at a spot right above us. "Right at the top of the stairs, away from anybody else."

"Ah," I say, nodding, looking up at the spot as if I'm a building inspector.

"You want to come up and trade stories of wishes, hopes, and desires?"

For a minute, I am thinking about it. I like Chellie King a lot. I like her dress a lot too. Liking her and considering what I might do about that, this is not a new thought for me. And now she's liking me too. And we have the cider in us, which covers a lot of the rough edges that could appear, tonight and tomorrow.

But I am a good guy. Sounds like crap, don't it? Sounds like crap to me too, but that still doesn't change the fact that it is, despite the occasional spasm, true. And there are probably a good fistful of reasons why a good guy would not do this, if he looked at it closely.

I don't much want to look at it closely, though.

"Now's the part, you know, Oakley, where you come in and make me forget all about the bad and the boring stuff. Y'know, like that."

Ah, Chellie King. There you go, Chellie King, you went and did it. There was something proposed a minute ago that I maybe could have done. This, though, is something I can't.

I step as close as I can to her—without touching her, because as I am finding out the gulf between being a good guy and being a real good guy is a mighty gaping gulf, oh boy.

"You know what?" I say, with a loaded wet sigh. "I can't make that trade. I'd be ripping you off."

She gives me a quizzical look, but she probably understands better than that. In fact, I'm sure she knows. I back away over the soft surface of the porch.

"Go inside now," I say. "A gentleman isn't supposed to leave a girl out in the nighttime."

"I can't believe, of all the rats around here, I had to pick the gent."

I like that, even if it isn't totally true. Especially because it isn't totally true. I wave her into the house anyway. I wait while she fumbles around in her coat pockets, pulling out crumpled Kleenex, dropping it onto the porch, pulling out a half pack of Hall's Mentholyptus, dropping it on the porch, pulling out the house keys. The door is open.

"Hey," she says, "all you did was confirm my faith in this dump anyway. So there." Chellie is waving, blowing a soft undramatic kiss that I'm sure I can feel land on the tip of my chin.

The door shuts, and I quick-step away, shaking my head.

Some people are hopeless.

# Everyone's Turned Out

EVERYONE HAS TURNED OUT. That's what they say, isn't it? Everyone's turned out for the funeral. She was such a fantastically well-regarded person that the whole town has turned out, plus relatives and pen pals and college chums from all over. Because that's what people do, I suppose, is they turn out. For funerals. Especially here. They turn out in droves here, in tribes and columns and gangs here, because we do beautiful funerals, for beautiful librarians, in Whitechurch.

But the truth is I wouldn't know who has turned out for the funeral of Ophelia Lennon and I wouldn't give a shit who has either. Don't notice. Don't care.

The library has been closed for four days leading up to and including the burial day itself, Saturday. Today. Would have been closed today anyway because it never opens on Saturday but if it did open Saturdays it wouldn't open on this one. Because Ophelia Lennon's not here. Ophelia Lennon was the library.

She was other things too. Right, everybody is other things too. Mr. King is the owner of the diner and he's Chellie's dad. The Reverend is the Reverend, god's assistant and all that and he's also father of that kid Lilly minds who can sometimes be a brat. And the Rev is a gun aficionado. And like that, so really everybody is more than they are, aren't they.

They should have opened it anyway, I think. The library is really the nicest place in town, and what better place to sit and think and pay, like, a tribute to Ophelia Lennon than the library? The funeral home? Chomskys' Funeral Parlor? Right, where the brothers Chomsky can follow you around and look sad because looking sad and asking if there's anything they can do is their job so you can be sure if you ask one of the professionally sad Chomsky brothers to do something seeing as they feel so bad and all they will do it for you and put it on your fucking tab. We are one big extended family here in town after all.

Or the church. The famous white Whitechurch church. Ophelia Lennon was never comforted by the place, so why would her fans be?

No, the library makes sense. That's a thing, isn't it, making *sense* of death? Aren't people always going on about "making sense" of death, or coping with "senseless" deaths? Well the library would do that. Open up the beautiful mahogany-crammed warm open-plan reading room where every single person was always comfortable and welcome before, where you could just sit and do nothing or nap or browse or write and you didn't have to know books or even like books or even know how to read in order to *get it* about the whole library thing. I heard it myself plenty of times, Ophelia Lennon sitting there reading to somebody too blind or lost or lonely to do it for himself. The only building in town where grown adults could get themselves read to, other than the church. And at the library you didn't have to be read to about the blackness of your soul.

Could've just opened it up and not worried about it at all, left the windows up and the lights on and I would just bet you that not a single person would cause trouble, that all the books would be refiled according to the Dewey decimal system or at least to the best of Whitechurch's ability—which was always fine enough for Ophelia Lennon who I think enjoyed the challenge of not only filing books properly, but of unfiling what we had done.

That would be the extent of the filing. No filing past the casket to view the body. No filing somberly into and out of church, no file of cars with orange flags following each other to the cemetery, as if we couldn't every one of us find our way there privately. What we would do that would make more sense would be to enter the library, browse, pick out an old favorite like *Winesburg, Ohio* or *Leaves of Grass*, read a short passage, and then be on our way. Would that not be a fair tribute to a librarian? Would that not make a librarian happy?

And I would bet everything that in four days nobody would have to shush anybody else in the Whitechurch Library.

But they did not open up the library for the occasion. Those kind of things don't happen. They did Chomskys' and the church, and everybody's by now turned out for at least part of it. Except me.

"Yo," Pauly says, standing at the wall of glass that takes up so much of the library's face.

"Yo," I say from the other side of the glass.

"I want you to let me in," he says.

"I don't want to let you in."

"Then I want you to come out."

"If I wanted to be out, I wouldn't have gotten in."

"Anyway, how'd you do that?"

"Let myself in," I say. "Have my own set of keys." A sudden maybe perverse but maybe not wave of pride comes over me. I say it again. "I have my own set of keys. Like I own the place. Did you know that, Pauly? Had 'em for years. What do you think of that?"

There is a pause, then a nod from Pauly. "I think that's great, Oak. I think that's the balls."

There is a pause, from me. "Ya, isn't it."

"Come on, Oakley, let me in. I swear I won't

do a thing I'm not supposed to, once you tell me what I'm not supposed to. I just think I should, you know, hang around with you."

I go quiet like I'm thinking about it, only I'm not thinking about it. "Sorry. Our hours are posted on the front door. Please come back during regular library hours." I pull closed the semi-sheer curtain between us.

"Come on, Oakley, you know I understand. I'm a poet, remember?"

I whip the curtain back open again, and point my finger at his face. "Don't. Don't you dare, Pauly. Not today."

"Maybe you'll like it. In fact, I know you'll—"

"Go away," I snap. I close the curtain and march away from the window. He is tapping and tapping away at it, but I cannot return, not right now.

I have barely reached the little room Ophelia Lennon called "the snug" when I hear more tapping. The snug is the coziest of reading rooms, with six upholstered tub chairs randomly placed around an oval teak coffee table. The snug was used for book discussion groups and meetings, for preschool story hour and after-school study hall. But mostly all anybody did was make up some nonsense excuse to get in there because more than anything else the snug was just like it sounds. Snug. More than any place you could imagine, this was snug. Kids have been known to seep into the snug and not come out for whole days. Fact.

There is a tall thin sofa table along one wall as you enter, and it was used for the coffeemaker and scones and the like when there was a group in there. When you were alone, it was the place where a certain strong scent would cause you to look up and find that a cup of banana tea and a piece of anisette toast had appeared out of nowhere. The room still smells like banana tea and anisette toast.

Still the knocking. One of the things that help the snug be snug is that there is but one window, and it is miniature and way high up. Like a basement window. So nobody could ever be looking in on you. And if they even wanted to knock they had to find a tree branch to do it. Like now.

"Leave me alone, Lilly."

"No, I won't."

"Ya, you will."

"Ah, no, I won't."

"I have a gun in here."

"You do like hell have a gun in there."

"Lilly, really, please just leave me be. Okay?"

"No, I don't understand, Oakley."

"You don't have to understand. You just have to fuck off."

That was a mistake. I know that was a mistake. I knew it was a mistake before I said it, but I said it anyway. Might say it again too, if she wants to keep this up.

"I'm sorry," she says. "Besides fucking off, is there anything else I can do?"

"No. That'll be enough. Thanks, Lil."

I listen for what goes on out there, and there is nothing. Which is good. If she were pretending to leave I'd hear something, like her throwing down the stick or the exaggerated shuffling of the feet. Lilly does the right thing. Of course.

As do I. I go for a browse.

I walk first, just for the exercise. I go a lap, and a lap feels good so I go another lap. As I do the second lap of the periphery of the big room, I get a little bolder touching things, running my finger along small statues and shelves and spines of books and if you think this is a dusty old library, that Ophelia Lennon maintained a library that had one speck of dust settled any-where near her titles, then you are wrong. My finger is cleaner after I swipe it over books than before.

Third lap I can stop. I can select titles. I can pull any one, I am sure, and she will have told me something about what is in there. I pull out *Tender Is the Night*. "The dew was still on her" comes to mind even though I never read it. She loved that one like nuts, said it every chance. I gently replace *Tender Is the Night*. It will not have to be refiled.

I go to the Religion section and pull out the King James Bible. "Judge not, that ye be not judged." There is a nice echo in here, just enough to make the Sermon on the Mount sound godly even in my voice. Or hers. Or hers. Even though she was really more of an Ecclesiastes fan.

I had forgotten how good books feel. Soft and

padded-leathery, the books in the Whitechurch lending library were treated more like show horses than lifeless things. They had a smell, like they'd always been recently rubbed down with mink oil or something keeping them all buttery. Very few volumes made a crackly sound when you open them. Forever young, her books were supposed to be, and it feels now like she almost did it. The look and feel and smell of everything here now reminds me so close of when I used to read.

I hate poetry. John Donne I hate. Probably more than the rest, but the competition is stiff. "Ask not for whom the bell tolls." Fine, John, I won't. Liars, poets. Phonies or jackasses or tricksters, but for sure fucking liars like John fucking Donne. Death be not fucking proud. As if it matters whether death is fucking proud or fucking ashamed of itself like it should be. "One short sleep past, we wake eternally." Really, John. Do tell, John. Thanks for clueing us, John. No really, thanks. "And death shall be no more; death, thou shalt die."

"Seems to me, John, that death is still here, but the ladies who read me your poems are gone."

Think of the time I wasted.

"Who you got in there with you?" Pauly calls from the front of the building.

"I told you to go away, Paul."

"I did. Now I came back."

"Excellent, so now you know the way. 'Bye."

"You ready to hear, Oakley?"

"This is really a good time for you to be gone, Pauly. Thanks and everything. But go, okay?"

"That's not what you want."

"That's what I want."

"Ya, but that's not really what you want. C'mon, Oakley, this is me. I know you. You should have me here."

I am certain I am slow deep-breathing loud enough for him to hear it out on the sidewalk. "Don't take this personally, ya psychotic bastard, but really you are of no use to me. Useless, you know the term? So what I want is for you to go as far away as you can. Can you do that? If I slow it down, a lot, and repeat it very very carefully for you, do you think you could manage to go? *Away?*"

He is of course gone already before I get to the slowed-down version. And I don't care.

I sit at Ophelia Lennon's desk, which sits in the center of the Whitechurch Library. It is a very old oak desk chair that sits on four tiny wheels of I think three different sizes. It is made comfortable, though, by pink-velvet seat cushions, secured with short shoestring-like ties. When I swivel, the chair whines out a dry small cry. I swivel some more and some more, seeing every bit of the library pass before me once and twice and thrice.

She was the only person I knew in this world who regularly used the word "thrice." I swear she maneuvered conversations to get that word in.

Thrice.

It's an excellent word, and I don't know why I don't use it more.

I pull open Ophelia Lennon's desk drawer. And I cannot bear Ophelia Lennon's desk drawer. Tea bags and stubby yellow pencils and recent and very not-recent issues of dull-as-dirt professional library journals, some of them with her name, Ophelia Lennon, on that little white address sticker, and some with the name of the previous head librarian still. Still. White hard mint candies with red diagonal stripes in clear cellophane with tightly twisted ends. If you were a kid in this library and you dared to sniffle, you got one of those. Likewise if you were an adult in this library. Likewise if you were any other sniffly snuffly being in this library. It was a very old tradition here.

I close the drawer and will never open it again.

I think about that. Maybe I will. There were once two librarians in the Whitechurch Library, once upon a fairy-tale time. Then there was one. And now there is not. Who knows what happens now? Who knows, the way things go? Maybe I should step into the job before the building itself goes gentle into that good night.

I've got the pedigree. But they may need somebody who reads books.

The phone rings. How 'bout this? Everybody in town is at the burial. Of the town's only librarian. Everybody except me. And I'm inside the library. And the phone rings. And the library wasn't even open on Saturdays even when the librarians were alive. I must say, when the phone rings in this very serious emptiness, I jump. But I answer.

Maybe it's one of them, I figure. Maybe it's a hot line, and I'm going to pick up and find one of them on the other end. The dead librarians of Whitechurch hot line.

"Oakley?" This is the only living person's voice I will tolerate at this moment. But I will tolerate it just barely, and just for a moment.

"Oakley," Lilly repeats. "I'm worried about you."

This brings a strange small smile to my painfully unsmiling face. "Worried? About *me*? I'm the sane one, remember?"

"Right. Well you can save that for all the people who don't know. I know better. And you are scaring me."

"Finally," I say, and in a way I am actually, truly pleased to hear this. "After all this time, finally you find me scary. That mean you love me now?"

"Loved you before," she says, and really I have no retort for that. Dead space. Dead air, over the phone line. That is my retort.

Lilly picks it up for both of us. "I baked," she says.

This is newsworthy. If it was not obituary-related baking, this would be front-page *Whitechurch Spire* material.

"You did *what*, Lilly?"

"Apple-blackberry torte, how's that?"

I kind of know what that means. It is infinitely sad to me.

"You baked."

"I baked."

"You taste it?"

"Yup. I worked really hard. Tastes like crap."

I am sure it does not. To my knowledge Lilly has never even turned an oven on before, much less commanded all the forces it must take to bake something from scratch. But I do not for a minute doubt that she did it, and probably did it okay.

"You didn't even know her, Lilly. You never even met—"

"I know you, though."

Here is where it's good to be on the phone, because I think now I'm going to do what I do not do. I think now I'm going to cry.

"So," she says after a respectful pause, "I'm gonna go to the house."

"Nnnhh," I say.

"Come with?"

This is so huge, and so impossible, I just get worse, and feel more and more stupid for it, but am speechless all the same. I shake my head into the phone.

"You shaking your head now, Oakley?"

I nod.

"I think you should come. I do. I'll be there, so it'll be all right."

I shake my head no.

"I think it'll be good for you. Maybe this is, like, the thing, the moment, you know? Your release, your walking papers, your diploma."

"No."

"Maybe this finally cuts the cord—"

"No."

"Breaks the chain—"

"No."

"I'm thinking of you, Oakley. I'm thinking you deserve better and more and stuff. Come with."

Come with. I'm thinking about "Come with" as I hang dumbly on the phone, and then it comes into view. The procession, filing past the library. The hearse. The flower car. The cars full of mostly older folks who can't do a lot of walking. Then the bulk of mourners, on foot. Spooks, the lot of them, floating past, through the haze of the gauze of the curtains of the library window. Then they stop, right out front.

"You see it," Lilly says.

I nod.

"Wish I was there with you."

I am crying so hard, such buckets of rain, I am frightened by it, like it's a medical problem that'll bleed me dead if I don't control it. I'm glad

Lilly is not here with me. I'm glad nobody is here with me.

It's Pauly's voice I hear now.

"Everybody knows you're in there, Oak. They're all talking about you like you're *me*. Don't want that now, do ya?"

I feel myself smile. Crying and smiling, which strikes me as Pauly enough. "Thrice now, Pauly. This is thrice I've had to tell you to leave me alone. Thrice."

"Come with?"

I shake my head.

"Okay then. We'll be you. Me and Lilly, we'll be you. Everybody will know that."

Why are they lingering so long out there?

"Wanna hear it now?" he says very softly.

I shake my head adamantly.

"There's no messin' here, Oak. It's the best thing I ever did. Not just the best poem. The best *thing* I ever did."

Still, there is no way. There is simply no way.

"Did you write it down?"

"Ya."

"Okay. Throw it in," I say. "Will you do that for us, Pauly? That's the thing. She would love it. I know she would love it and I love that she would love it. When the time comes, you throw it in with her."

Pauly agrees. I hang up.

Finally, finally, the procession gets itself started again, and I walk to the window behind the curtain and watch nearly every face I have ever known as they walk along, following the casket car carrying the body of Ophelia Lennon.

Up to the hill where they bury all the librarians and poetry of Whitechurch.

# SACREDS

I T'S ALL DARK, AND IT'S ALL QUIET, in a way
that is more than just the old after-hours
feeling. It always gets dark at night, and it
always gets quiet, even on Saturday eventually,
but weekend quiet has a feel to it like it isn't
noise, but you can definitely sense something is
going on. I don't get that feeling now. It's quiet-
quiet as I pass the burger and donut and pie
places, and as I pass Chuck's International Auto
Parts, and as I pass the Laundromat. I love this
quiet. I stop there at the dead center, the still,
unbeating heart of my petrified northern town. I
spread my fingers for the cold, watch my breath
curl slowly, more like smoke than steam, and I
smell the crystal, night smell that is the purest
thing about Whitechurch.

There is nothing at all still happening in this
town at this moment and the thought brings an

immense peace to me. Only then do I realize that I've been at something other than peace.

The empty coffee shop below my apartment, with its mocha fog aroma to lay me down and no people to mess it up, is now the most welcoming of thoughts as I come up on home.

"What are you doing out walking at this hour?" Lilly asks.

My heart rate is sent jackrabbitty. "Shit, Lilly," I say, putting a hand over my chest and spluttering like a horse through my lips.

She is sitting on the concrete step in front of the shop. "You do a lot of that now. Walking around. You trying to get someplace, my Oakley?"

I stare at her, lean toward her as if I just cannot make out what she is saying, even though I can make it out just fine. "If you weren't haunting my doorstep in the middle of the night, this wouldn't be an issue."

She grins up at me, like she knows everything, whether or not there is anything to know.

"I thought you had a date anyway," I say, taking a seat beside her.

"Jeez, now it's your turn. Shut up, will you?"

"Why, what's so wrong?"

"Oh, well, where to begin? Pauly spying on me, that's one. Then, there's you and your new restlessness giving me chills. And finally I'm out having a cup of tea with this strange boy who I'm thinking, okay, Lilly, he's cute, right, got the mystery thing going for him and all, and it turns out he is *so* gay he cannot even *speak* to me once it's just the two of us."

I'm laughing before she's even finished. The story makes me happier than I've been in a while and reminds me, again, that I've not been as happy as I thought.

"Go ahead, laugh. I'm like, forcing questions on him and he just keeps grunting, until finally he asks me if *Adam* is seeing anybody. Ya, he keeps going back and washing his clean clothes every week just to hang out at the 'mat."

I reach over and squeeze her hand, while we both laugh. "Finally," she says, "I just stopped walking to see if he'd mind—seeing as he was supposed to be walking me home and all. He never even slowed down. Far as I know he's still out there, walking in the dark someplace. The bum."

"Well, you can be a kind of intimidating babe, Lilly. Maybe you owe *him* an apology. Maybe he wasn't even gay till he got alone with *you*."

She turns to me. "Shut up, boy. Aren't you going to invite me upstairs for a drink?"

I stand right up. "Not unless you mean to be drinking with my old man."

"Thought your old man didn't drink anymore."

"That's a filthy rumor. Anyway, for you he'd make an exception."

"He's gotta be asleep now anyway."

"For you he'll get up."

Lilly extends a hand, and I pull her up by it. We begin walking westward, toward Lilly's house up on the other lip of the bowl.

"So you can offer *me* a drink when we get to *your* house, right?" I say.

She doesn't answer, doesn't need to. Lilly's parents are always home. Her two adult sisters are always home. And ever since she began dating Pauly, it appears that at least one of them is awake standing watch at all hours like it's an army installation. So this is a joke.

Once, it was a funny joke.

"So where do you go?" she says. "You go to the cemetery?"

"I go everyplace," I say. "I just go, and then I go some more."

We make our way along the quiet brittle street, out of the center of town, and begin the first few degrees of the climb out of Whitechurch. I slip again into that calm feeling, the feeling of nothing going on, that proved to be so wrong when Lilly spooked the life out of me. Anyway, having the feeling is more important than being right about it, and it's a groove and I'm liking it, liking it better in Lilly's presence too as she is the only person who can be there and not shatter solitude at the same time.

"So, you go for redheads," I say.

"No," she says.

"So, why?" I ask.

"I don't know."

We pass the modest square parish house

where the Reverend lives and where Lilly baby-sits. No mistaking the quiet of that. It is real quiet, the kind of quiet that embarrasses you. We continue on, past First Unitarian, into the valley of the shadow of the tower of the White Church.

For nothing, and from nowhere, it comes out.

"Pauly?" I say into the cold air.

"Ah, Oakley," she says sadly. She gets a wrinkled-up look, like she's trying hard to come up with a better answer than the truth. She shakes her head.

I suppose I'm not really surprised. But I can't suppress an involuntary heavy sigh. "Ah, Pauly."

Lilly veers.

"What are you doing?" I ask from the side-walk as she comes up to the large natural oak door of the church. "Suddenly you got an urge to pray?"

Lilly pulls keys out of her pocket. You can hear the bang of the tumblers of the biggest lock in town clear to the other end of the town. Lilly has the run of the place. She does this and that, polishing and sweeping and the like, and so the church is at her disposal. I find something cool and powerful and sexy about this, and love to visit her there, especially when the church is empty and she is sweeping and the hard bristle broom makes a loud, echo-y scratching sound that could just as easily be a steam locomotive if you close your eyes.

"Suddenly I do got an urge to pray," Lilly

says. "That okay with you?" She evanesces.

"Can't mess with a person's religion, I guess," I say, following into the church.

I close the door behind me to find myself in near-total darkness. I listen, know Lilly is in there, but the feathery sound she makes could just as easily be a mouse crossing the floor.

"You are a daring young man, Oakley-doakley," she calls out from the creepy dark.

"Am I?"

"Yes you are. He gets jealous enough when you're just dating me, but now you're in the church, in the middle of the night . . . that's like, his big fantasy. He's gonna see red. And he's gonna kick your ass."

This is an old joke, Pauly being jealous of me and Lilly. The oldest joke we have. There was a time when it was true followed by a time when it wasn't, then a time when it was. We have all said it and denied it so many times, the thing has grown all serpentine and swirled in on itself to where nobody even knows anymore. So it works best as a joke.

"Where are you?" I ask.

She doesn't say anything.

"You could turn on a light. I don't know this place like you do. You want me to hurt myself?"

One small light snaps to life halfway up to the altar. "No," Lilly says easily, "I don't want you to hurt yourself."

It's not even a light that is actually inside the main body of the church. It is spilling through the glass door of the small private worship room used for baptisms, small funerals, and when it's too cold to heat the cavernous church for a congregation of twelve on a February morning. But the pinkish light spilling out of it is enough, reaching everywhere and attaching itself to the white granite of the walls so that they all have a low incandescence of their own. Quiet, everywhere light. The visual equivalent of a hum.

Lilly crosses the width of the church, turns at the center aisle and walks toward the back, toward frozen me who can't help but just have a long look at the grace of her.

Who is she? I've known her forever, but not really, really.

Who is she? I've known all this, you know, for a long time.

Who is she? I don't know a damn thing.

When she finally finally reaches me, I'm shaking, with fear and other fine things.

"Remember when you were in here the other day, and I told you you could really let loose in here when the meter wasn't running?"

I nod. Good job, Oak.

"Remember then you couldn't think of anything?"

I nod. True, I couldn't think of a thing then.

"Well *I* did."

I have kissed Lilly before.

But not this. No.

Lilly's top lip is against my top lip, and her bottom lip is against my bottom lip, and our mouths are open possibly an inch. Our hands are hanging at our sides until I take hers and squeeze them as hard as I can. Breath, we are exchanging, rather than tongues or motion. I close my eyes even though that is the absolute last thing I want to do. She begins to move her head from side to side as if she's saying no but no is not what she's saying. She's creating small perfect frictions with her two separated lips rubbing so lightly my two separated lips.

"I use my imagination quite a bit," she says thoughtfully, into me.

There is a pause, as if I should be adding my thoughts on the subject. I don't believe I can.

"Anyway," Lilly says, "I think you almost have to, growing up in a place like this. You need to use your imagination fully. And I've gotten pretty good at it."

"I worry," I say, and the words take me by surprise.

Lilly kisses me. "Don't."

"About imagination. It makes trouble."

I kiss Lilly.

"You don't believe that, Oakley."

"Well, as much as I believe anything . . ."

"Really? Well believe this. As hard as I push, and wherever my mind goes, you know what I cannot imagine, Oakley?"

"I can't imagine, Lil."

"I can't imagine you ever not being my friend, no matter what happens."

I try to think of one more evasive, glib thing

to say. One more is all I'll need.

I haven't got one more.

Lilly takes off her coat, then, seeing me somewhat paralyzed, helps me off with mine. "Okay, Lilly" is what I say, maybe to what she's doing, maybe to the words, certainly to the truth of the whole situation. As she sort of tugs down the jacket, pulling it from the sleeves and letting it drop to the floor behind me, I lean into her, burrowing into her neck.

"Should we be doing this here, Lilly? Should we be doing it *anywhere*?"

"You know what I think, Oak? I think it is very very much time that what you should do should be decided by *you*. And I'm going to do likewise."

Pauly now tries to climb into my mind. Still one creepy unit, the three of us. I should be guilty here. I want to be guilty. It will make me feel better, to be guilty.

I grab Lilly's face very firmly in my hands, turn it toward me. She kisses me on the corner of my worried, downturned mouth. I reach up and touch her hair, looking at it, as if I've never felt hair before, because hers looks and feels totally foreign now.

"I should go, maybe," I say. "I should walk you home. How many guys is it gonna take to get you walked home tonight anyway?"

"I've spent a lot of hours in here, Oak, and I've thought about this as much as anyone who ever sat in these pews."

"I've sat in these pews. I don't know what was I thinking about."

"And I've seen the church in its underwear if you know what I mean. I have respect, y'know, and I appreciate what it means to worship, if you know how, and I think that most people don't really know how."

"I don't think I ever knew how, Lil."

"And I know what 'sacred' means."

"And I really wish I did. Pauly, he was always *trying*, at least, but I never knew what I was doing. . . ."

We sit down on the red carpeted floor, hip-to-hip and facing opposite directions. A small tilt of the head puts us once more face-in-face.

"Pauly hasn't got a clue what 'sacred' means," Lilly says. "But you do."

"I do?" I ask, closing one eye on her.

A quick small breath comes out of her.

"You look like Pauly right now," she says.

"I was just about to tell you the same thing."

I do the leaning, then press my mouth against hers just as I finish speaking. I adore this feeling, more than anything I have ever felt, the sensation of talking right up against Lilly's mouth, of talking into Lilly. I don't need anything else. This is *it* for me, and all other parts of this may be great, but I know they will not be greater than this. They will not need to be.

# MUCK

Gotta get up,
Pauly says right into my ear.
Right now,
gotta get up,
gotta show ya something.
Damn, Pauly, I say,
rolling away from him,
propping myself up
and staring,
like a thing cornered,
eyes wide but blurred.
Pauly's eyes no better.
Hasn't been to bed, and
wet red rims

halo dilated pupils.

The rank of all the muck that's inside him,

the peculiar chemical hormonal stew,

that always comes with him

when things are happening,

what he likes to call

desperation perspiration

fills my apartment,

overpowers even the coffee scent.

You don't have to show me nothing right now,
    Pauly.

Pauly snatches the bed covers and tears them
    away.

Yes I do,

right now.

It might not be there later.

Maybe, I say tentatively,

pulling my blankets back up over me,

you don't have to show me at all.

Maybe you could just tell me about it,

or maybe even not.

Pauly goes all calm.

I could just dress you myself,

but that would be kind of undignified

for both of us,

don't you think?

Pass me my pants over there.

Pauly talks, sitting on the end of the bed, while
    I dress.

Tell me about last night, he says.

You look like you had a good

last night.

I snap up, zip up, pull on my boots without
    socks.

What does a look like that look like?

Tell me all, says Paul.

Come on, Oak.

Pauly is no longer

grim and cryptic.

C'mon, c'mon,

guys tell.

Friends tell.

Decent folks don't.

Decent folks don't, he repeats,

and is big-time amused

by the sound.

As I reach the bottom

of the stairs,

Pauly comes up behind me,

grabs me in a hug

that carries us

right out onto the frosted sidewalk.

Pauly's chin is resting on my shoulder,

as if we were one

two-headed beast.

Thank you. He says.

But why don't you tell me anyway.

I tell *you* everything.

If I even have a thought,

I tell you about it.

Whether I want you to or not.

Exactly.

No secrets between us,

ever.

I'm taking you to see my surprise right now,

am I not?

Which I have a strong feeling I don't want to
     see.

I pull away, banging Paul hard in the chin with
     my shoulder.

Paul lays a hand on his chin.

Which way are we going,

and how the hell did you get in my house
     anyway?

We're going that way,

toward the train station,

and your place is the easiest building
in all of Whitechurch
to get into.
Sometimes I let myself in
when you're sleeping,
I come in,
don't even wake you up,
stare at you a bit,
then I go out again.
Just to do it.
Lie.
No lie.
We walk down Main,
into the crux of the town,
cut up Station Street to the north.
Up the hills again,
the famed seven hills of Whitechurch.
Up one of them anyway.
Until we have reached
over the north lip of the bowl
and down again,
where the land flattens
and the Victorian station rises
with its rusted iron lamps
still lit,

its bleached wooden platform
empty and exposed.
We stand there, freezing.
I'm freezing anyway,
Pauly shows no sign.
As we look all around
the dead-Sunday-morning depot,
looking like we've seen it look
a billion other times.
This isn't what you wanted to show me, Paul.
Paul shakes his head,
pulls me by the jacket.
We walk out onto the platform,
jump down onto the tracks.
We cross the tracks,
enter the immediate, dense woods
of maple and fir,
shocks of white birch and
blurs of blue spruce.
We travel on
for another hundred yards or so
until Pauly stops dead,
and starts growling
like a dog.
What? I say, as this is strange stuff

even for Paul,

and rush up beside him to look.

I look while Pauly growls.

Ah . . . no, Paul . . .

The words barely get airborne

as the life

drains from my belly.

The Stranger is lying,

in a spot

where campfires often burn.

There is a broad circle of round white stones

ringing him entirely,

and another

leaning against his cheek.

There is one visible injury on him

but one

seems to be plenty.

It is impossible to see

a left eye,

in the socket

pressed against the rock.

I drop to a seat on a large stone,

grabbing two handfuls

of my own hair

for, I don't know,

support,
grounding.
Lilly didn't come home last night,
Paul says,
flatly informational.
I hung by her house till four thirty this morning.
I cannot let go of the tight grip of the hair, or
the head and hands
will both shake
insanely.
You knew, Paul.
Never once asked her
not to.
I was just testing, he says, again, sounding
almost rational,
as if he's surprised
there is any confusion
over this.
Maybe you should stop
testing
people
Pauly.
Maybe it's fucking time
you stopped.
He shakes his head.

That's how you find things out.
The only way to really know
anything.
He gestures,
with an upturned open hand,
at the Red-Headed Stranger.
A guy doesn't do
that kind of a thing.
This guy here, he's got no damn respect.
You just don't come along . . .
he didn't even walk her home,
which I think is what made me maddest.
Four thirty, I gave up,
went out looking,
found him
just out buzzin' around town,
like he ain't even satisfied yet
and he's lookin' for more.
With a snap of his head, Pauly's now looking at
    his
lifelong friend
who is me.
He found it, though,
didn't he, boy?
He was lookin' for *more*,

and he sure got that,
didn't he,
Oakley-doakley?
My eyes are closing,
on their own,
and I can feel the roots of my hairs
letting go of the scalp.

I wonder if Lilly will even ever know. Sure she
    will,
sometime,
but probably not today or this week because
    she is gone,
was gone,
before Pauly even came to get me,
I imagine.
Already packed up and hitched, most likely.
South to Boston
would be the thinking,
what with the college visit and her having made
    up her mind and
not likely to change just like that.
That would be the thinking,
but I'm thinking
probably otherwise.

I'm thinking she points west.
I'm thinking she never really did mean
to go to Boston,
but meant to do it
more or less exactly
the way she did it,
leaving no tracks,
and when she's ready,
if she is ready,
she'll take a look back over her shoulder and
    maybe be in touch.
And maybe
not.
And I wonder
if Pauly will ever even know
but then do we really wonder
for one second
that Pauly ever *didn't* know?
Pauly knew before it was even true.
They will want to talk to me,
but nobody is going to ask
me about me
because I am Oakley
and Pauly is Pauly
and who cares
in the end?

They will be looking into the Red-Headed
    Stranger
and finding out
RHS was really John Wesley Harding
and he had a whole set of his own things
to be running from,
from his own place
which brought him to
our place,
which was
his loss.
His
loss.
His. Funny, no?
How one person's grave misfortune
which should have been mine
can mean
almost nothing,
to me.
I feel
almost nothing.
Funny, no.
Sentenced to Whitechurch,
he calls out the Dodge Ram window,
heading up over the southern rim
of the Whitechurch bowl,

past the prison.
The town is still sleeping.
The train station
won't open
till tomorrow,
so he'll get a good jump.
Before they catch him
in Boston.
He never even asked me to go with him.
And when they bring him back they will want
    to talk.
But I don't want to talk
about poets
and the muck that's inside us
anymore.
So I will be gone
finally
over the northern rim of the bowl
to say
nothing,
to do
something,
and to feel
like feeling.

*   *   *

Give us the kiss
make it all
better
better
yet
give us the smile.